AF483392

STORIES • MAX HIPP

These short stories are works of fiction. Names, characters, places, situations, and events are either works of imagination or mangled and misremembered facts.

What Doesn't Kill You Opens Your Heart
by Max Hipp

Published 2024 by Cool Dog Sound, LLC

P.O. Box 454 • Water Valley, MS 38965
www.cooldogsound.com

For more information contact
maxbhipp@gmail.com or dozens@cooldogsound.com

Stories in this volume originally appeared in slightly different forms in the following literary journals: "How to Pick Up Beautiful Women" & "Disciples of Suede" in *Bull*, "Last Year's Man" in *7x7*, "Stump Girl" in *Southern Humanities Review*, and "Death May Be Your Santa Claus" in *Pontoon*.

ISBN 979-8-218-37795-3 (paperback)

Cover and book design by Susan Bauer Lee
Author photograph by Tracy Morin

CONTENTS

To my father in his eightieth year,
and to my mother, the reading champion.

STUMP GIRL

Slick T camps in the woods not fifty yards off 328 because no one will house him anymore, not even me. He shows up eerie silent on Saturday morning sporting his fishing vest, nothing beneath it, and khakis streaked with ditch clay.

By ten thirty, we reach the lake out on Daddy's land. We flip the boat over and step back for wasps and cottonmouths, then paddle to where the bass grow fat on sunk Christmas trees. Pre-drunk, my mind loops over my ex-wife Sara's dimples, her goober nose. My thoughts swing to my drunk ravings and cravings, our lost marriage, how I ruined what tiny happiness we'd carved into the world.

Slick T says, "I left a girl in the woods, Boss," like he's lost his keys. "I got blackout drunk and left her on a stump." He shivers. "Think maybe I killed her."

His girl on the stump shakes something loose in me. This muffled hum starts in my ear like a gnat burrowing in honey. He's had scrapes with the law and is out of get-out-of-jail-free cards. Drunk car crashes, knocking people up. Maybe it was just a matter of time before he killed somebody.

"You've lost your damn mind," I say. "You did no such thing." My line clicks as I reel it in empty. I just want to fish, and he comes at me with stump girls.

On his next cast, the end of his pole slaps into the water, and he kneels on the seat for it, cussing. My foot in his ass flops him face-first into the water.

He comes up puffing and sputtering.

"It's like you farted in my church," I say. I throw my beer at him. "I should club you with this paddle."

He stands up, water to his waist. "I wish you would."

A crow squawks overhead and lights in a dead pin oak.

"We're going," I say. "You scared the fish."

Back in the boat, the vest clings to his spine as he paddles. It feels like the beginning of the end of everything.

Raccoons have spread his garbage everywhere, Wonder Bread and Cheetos bags blown into the briars. He takes a long drink from a water jug and roots around in his tent for his pocketknife until I make him show me where he left the girl.

We follow what looks like a deer trail. Sometimes I think the trail has ended, but Slick T keeps going. I'm thankful it's too early for ticks and mosquitoes and poison ivy. We climb down red banks to a clearing with an enormous stump, a long-gone white oak. He drops to his knees, eyes closed.

There's no girl. I want to weep. He's annoyed me for entire years of my life. I lose it and kick him in the chest. Sara might still be my wife if Slick T didn't need so much help. Fresh from a bender, I signed her divorce papers.

"I left her right here, Boss!" he hisses from the ground.

I stomp the briars back to my truck. Slick T hates himself for how life turned out. How he was too drunk to help his mother's dementia when she blasted shotgun holes through the sheetrock of their old home place. How he couldn't stop the bankruptcy or foreclosure from doctor bills.

By the time I get home, I'm hammered with the truth of getting old, the losing of so much love. I grab a fresh handle of gin and walk out to the backyard naked, feel the night's breath on my junk. Crickets scream as stars reveal themselves like lovers. The wind picks up sweet honeysuckle wafts from the woods. I remember Sara's pursed lips under that goober nose.

I swear before I pass out, a stump girl, her face luminous smoke, meanders out of the bushes.

I hit the factory floor on Monday with my shoes untied, don't even bother, just tuck the laces in. We pour burnt-orange liquid into molds shaped like jack-o'-lantern faces, wait twenty minutes, and pull out pottery. My job is to snatch them, stinging hot from the chemicals, and make sure the triangle eyes are carved out, the mouths gap-toothed, and the bottoms trimmed. Someone can put a candle inside, so the theory goes, and this is considered attractive. I work thousands of these pieces of shit with a cheap knife and wonder who would buy such a thing. Sometimes they come out deformed, faces missing or the corners chipped and flaking. That's when I smash them onto the shard heaps under the tables. I take great pleasure in smashing them. Some days, what I do most is smash things.

It's shameful, but I drive by Sara's house after work and park in the duplex a few driveways down. She comes out in tights and a sports bra, too heartbreaking to be in public, and begins to run.

My heart clogs with sand and wet newspaper.

Once she gets past the big houses on the hill, I slide down side streets to avoid detection. I only wanted her to be herself, never asked her to change, and made it clear I'd never change. But as she turns the corner, I think maybe I've never seen either of us clearly.

Our former selves were blurs, but now the focus is too sharp. Or maybe she's sharp, and I'm still dull.

I get caught at a light. I drive toward the university, but the streets are empty of runners, and Sara's another lost girl.

I watch baseball and get evil drunk on freezer gin. In the backyard, I pull up fistfuls of grass, kick over lawn furniture that hasn't been used in the year since Sara left. We'd have couples over to barbecue, her friends, respectable people who smiled and talked to me like I was worth a damn when I was making construction money. Now when I see those people in town, I duck around corners. I don't enjoy the what-are-you-doing-now question or the I-work-in-a-pottery-factory answer.

The whole town knows Slick T isn't all there. In the beginning, the cops would pick him up just for fun. That went on until he shat in the back of a patrol car. Since then, it's been a war, if you can have a war where one side is all guns and muscle and the other side has nothing but a fishing vest.

Sara hated Slick T, hated the way he lives, and never understood what I see in him. I've explained Little League championships, how we're like brothers strung together through blood and muck. I told her about our best years framing houses, both of us thinking we were courageous men setting straight the crooked world instead of knocking it out of true. She'd smile at that and say nothing because she's smarter than me. Within seven months of getting married, she knew I was a goner.

I go inside and put on a bathrobe.

Even though I know she doesn't exist, I picture the stump girl, brown leaves piling around her, her face made up like girls who want to look old enough to get into bars and run into people like Slick T. Ugly as he is, he has a way with those girls, always has, since he was young and dumb and full of you-know-what.

Next day, I wear a mask to heft hundred-pound bags of dust into a mixer shaped like a horse trough where metal blades combine it with water and whip it into chocolate milk that smells like clay. It's a hundred degrees in the room. White dust coats the walls and gums my eyelashes. After my shift, I leave without even air-hosing off.

Sara passes me on the highway going the other direction. I U-turn to follow her through town until she pulls into a strip mall and gets out dressed in a karate outfit, a blue belt, and goes into Isshinryu Dan's Karate World.

All the lights are on inside, lots of windows so I can see everything from where I park. They get in formation and follow the sensei, kick and punch at the mirror behind him. Sara punches and kicks. She throws people. They throw her. She keeps getting up and shaking it off, and I realize she's a completely different organism since she left me. I thought she needed a man, even one like me, but it isn't true. Sitting in my car in the parking lot, I feel sickly lonely.

At the end of class, everybody bows and smiles. Sara's face is shiny, pink, happy. It's like they've been through something awful but the struggle was worth it. I ask myself if the factory and living out the shards of a life is worth it, the leaf blowers howling emptiness through my soul.

Sweaty Sara glides to her car. Her headlights sweep into traffic, and the sun dips behind the strip mall. The town darkens me.

I leave work at three thirty again, covered in dust, wanting a beer and a cool, dark place to drink it. Slick T is on my porch.

"I'm sorry, Boss."

"I'm not worried about it."

He's smoked his cigarette down to a filter wedged and forgotten between his fingers.

"I thought for sure I'd killed her. I don't know what's the matter with me."

"Does she have a name you could look up? A phone you could call?"

"I blacked out anything else. I was thinking maybe I left her in town. I guess she's just a dead girl on the brain."

She appears then at my tree line like a flashbulb dying out, her long, wavy hair thick as a billion spider legs. My tailbone purrs. She places a finger to her lips and fades.

"Nah," I say, shaking. "If she's anywhere, she's on a stump out in the woods."

He's wide-eyed, like I'm god speaking and he hears the clarion call.

That night, I roll around on the floor with the empties I pushed off the coffee table and think of stump girl, leaves up to her shoulders, her painted face wearing an expression like life is a joke not worth telling. Turkey vultures preen on bare boughs around her.

Somehow I make it through the rest of the week without bothering anyone.

On Saturday, Slick T sets up the poles, and we fish again. Because we don't catch anything, we drink more. Because we drink more, we go drinking afterward.

Barney's Tavern is overrun with frat boys and girls dressed like cartoon hippies. Tie-dyed shirts and bell-bottom jeans and John Lennon glasses. The bartender slaps down change, flashes the peace sign.

Max Hipp

"I'm sick of this missing girl I killed," Slick T says. "I've been telling everybody about her."

"Don't spread that around."

"Too late," he says. "It's spread."

I shake my head and order another round of whiskey shots and beers to chase them. Sara keeps haunting me, and she's not even popping out of the woods like stump girl to stare me down.

When Slick T gets up to scam kids at pool, I leave and go straight to her house. I pull up and honk until the light comes on inside. I get out and lean, act natural.

The front door opens. She's wearing her gi with the belt tight around the waist. She disappears in the shade of the magnolia, clatters dead leaves, reappears on the sidewalk under the streetlight. Up close, I can tell she's been taking care of herself, drinking those healthy drinks. Her eyes bright and wild, she takes a fighting pose.

Next thing I know, I'm on my back in the street with her looming over me.

"Don't come to my house. You hear me?"

I try to say yes but have no breath for it. The punch spreads like her knuckles went through my stomach and knocked my spine loose. I struggle to sit up and gasp, and I puke all over my tire.

"I had enough of your drunk bullshit when we were together. You keep following me, calling me, or showing up here, I'm going to knock your teeth out."

I spit out the last of the puke and nod, my eyes watering.

She starts to walk off, then comes back.

"Let me ask you. Do you think you can just do and say whatever you want and nothing will happen to you?"

I try to mull it over, but there's too much pain.

"You're almost forty. Grow up."

Cold sweat runs down my temples like I'm getting the flu.

"I'm rooting for you, Boss," she says.

She goes in and slams the deadbolt home.

Now I know exactly where to find stump girl.

Her white legs dangle off the stump in the woods behind my house. I wade through leaves right to her. Naked as she could possibly be, she sits up with purple lips. White pupils and irises float in black pools.

"I've been waiting for you." Her mouth doesn't move. Her eyes are what's speaking. Her voice resonates through the toilet-paper tubes of my heart.

Stump girl knows my insides. I tell her I'm terrified. I say, "I've never been right in my life." And it hits me, man, the bottom. The truth is rock bottom.

She looks through me a moment, blinks, and lies down to drink the stars.

I back out of there, crash through the briars, getting scratched and welted, and make it to bed before dawn. Maybe I sleep.

My body vibrates like a struck bell.

I go to the brick jail with the high, narrow windows. When I tell the lady who I'm there to see, she gives me the stink eye. After forever, a jailer shows me to a cinderblock visiting room.

Slick T's ex-wife waited three days to call and tell me the cops took him to county and charged him with murder. For a few hours, I worried I might've called the police in my fever, but I talked to a bartender friend who said Slick T told everyone in the bar where I left him that he killed a girl. Somebody finally got spooked about the lunatic in the fishing vest.

Slick T comes and sits behind the Plexiglas. He's cleaned up and clear-eyed, looking good in the starched orange jumpsuit, like he's found his place in the world.

"Man," he says, "you look like shit."

I want to tell him stump girl is in the woods behind my place. Not dead, but not alive either. She's still ringing in me. "We're going to get you out of here," I say instead. "I can't lose you."

"Hush." He shakes his head. "It's okay, Boss. I've been prepping for this my whole life." He half grins to reassure me.

There's no body, no motive, no murder weapon, no witness. There's only his confession and whether or not the cops want to keep him. He doesn't have money to grease the gears of justice. His mistake is never leaving the place he was born, which makes his list of enemies a mile long.

I'm light-headed leaving the jail.

Stump girl is standing in the backyard when I pull up. Fear screws me to the landscape. There's something she demands of me even as she thins and rises like chimney smoke.

That night, after some liquid courage, I agree to the terms of Sara's punishment.

The windows are dark. I honk until the blinds part and the porchlight comes on. I get out and lean against the truck.

The front door opens: Sara lamplit in the threshold. She double knots the blue belt around her waist. I feel the warm hum rising in me like I'm the mouthpiece of the trumpet of the world.

BLOOD & STARS

illy and Vonda eat dinner and stop at Itchy's where college girls are dancing to a Tom Petty cover band while huddled boys buy whiskeys and watch. Billy notices they let the ice melt and drink it watered down. Sometimes they forget their drinks entirely, like the money and dancing will never end.

When it gets too loud to sit by the bar, they switch to a table at the back of the room. Vonda peels the label off her bottle and smooths it back sideways with her thumb. She's in a black blouse and a jean skirt that stops just above her knees. Even in her check-out lane at Big Star, in a faded blue t-shirt with a nametag, she was like a neon arrow beside a dark highway. Billy realized he'd been in a darkness. He asked her out right there, with a line of buggies behind him.

"Tell me the worst thing about you," she says, still wearing the kind smile. Her silver pendant swings as she repositions herself on the stool. "Might as well start with it."

Billy rocks back. He tells himself she isn't asking about the slivers of moon across his knuckles. She isn't asking about the angry line down the inside of his wrist from when drunk-ass Hopkins hit him head-on, and the deputies placed a white bag over Hopkins' daughter without zipping it. She isn't asking about any of that, so there's no need to sink this date with it.

"The worst thing right now is I need to make more money." He needs a whiskey too but senses, somehow, Vonda wouldn't like that. Her creamy eyeshadow makes him wish he was the kind of guy who could stop after two beers without giving it another thought.

"Shit," she says, "I've been letting you pay for everything."

He shakes his head. "My restaurant gig pays okay. It's just hard to find work around here that's not in a restaurant or Wal-Mart."

"If I didn't live with Mom, I don't know where I'd be. And if that's the worst, you're doing good." Beer lights glitter in her eyes. "Your luck's going to change."

They chink bottles to luck. She brushes some specks off her sleeve. At her house, Billy sat with her mother and Emily, Vonda's three-year-old daughter, across from a flat-screen showing the Christian Broadcasting Network, until she came out of the bathroom.

"Your turn," he says. "Tell me the worst about you."

"Emily's daddy. My ex." She takes a long swig. "He wanted to take his childhood out on me."

Billy's own childhood unrolls in his mind like a rug full of dog hair and cigarette butts. By the time he was five, he wished he was grown. "I'm sorry to hear it."

"That feels like a whole different life, almost like the bad times happened to another person." Vonda glances at one of the muted screens over the bar. "Other days, though, I worry maybe nothing changes much."

The kitchen jobs blur together in Billy's memory. The buckets of slop no one wants, the plates banging against the plastic until the food slides off. "It's funny how the past gets like that. You get further from it and it's different. Only it doesn't really change. Just seems to because you've changed."

She squints at him. "I like the way you think."

He nearly coughs out beer. "You might be the first person who's ever said that."

The band takes a break. The college students clear the room to smoke cigarettes on the balcony. Seeing college kids have fun always makes him feel like he's missed something. He had a baseball scholarship lined up before the wreck. A free ride. Pushing thirty now in the town where he grew up, he tries not to hate them as they cross the dance floor with fresh drinks, the way they seem to own the world.

Vonda cradles her chin, elbows propped on the table, eyebrows raised like she can't wait to give him a present. Sitting with her is so much nicer than the empty bottles and paper plates all over his rented apartment, the roaches scuttling across the counter when he flips on the kitchen light.

"I haven't been out much since I've had Emily," she says. "Just working and going home and hanging out with Mom and baby girl most weekends. I haven't missed this."

A drunk boy in a too-big suit falls off a stool and lands flat on his back, laughing. His friends gather around to help him up.

She touches Billy's arm. "Not that I'm not having a good time."

"I know what you mean," he says. He finishes his beer.

When they arrived at Itchy's, she said she had time for just one drink. He chews his tongue, fixates on another but figures it's best that he doesn't get it.

He drives down County Road 465, Vonda's face serene in the radio lights like a girl in a film about Paris, Texas he found at the public library. The girl remained mysterious, in home movies and behind glass for most of the film, and he fell a little in love with her.

Vonda's scent, clean and sweet, reminds him of his mother's arm around him in the church pews on Sunday mornings.

They come around the last bend before her house. A Honda Fit with its lights off is parked in front of her driveway. "It's goddamn Pete," she says. Her body stiffens. She covers her face, peers through her fingers. "He's probably drunk."

Fear rises in Billy's guts and he wishes he'd had a few more beers before this drive. Now the night, like most nights, won't end well. For some reason, nothing he does ends well, but whatever happens is going to happen one way or another and they might as well get on with it. He pulls over, keeps the lights on and the truck idling when they get out.

Pete climbs from his muddy car with a beer bottle, wearing jeans and a white undershirt, a baseball cap pulled low. Billy is relieved he isn't any taller, just carries a few more pounds of beer belly.

"Who's this?" Pete says.

"This is Billy."

"Pleased to meet you," Billy says.

"Fuck you. I ain't here to meet you. You're out with my wife." Pete turns up the backwash and chucks the bottle into the field, never taking his eyes off them. "Did you fuck him?"

"We went to dinner," she says.

"Not that it's any of your business," Billy adds.

"Motherfucker, you shut your mouth. This is husband and wife shit."

"Ex-husband," she says. "Ex-wife."

Billy keeps his hands in his pockets and glares at Pete, who reminds him of players he pitched against, ones who whined to the umpires about called strikes. Ones who talked shit and pissed their pants when confronted.

"If I call the police they'll take you away this time."

"I know about your piece of paper," he says. He turns to Billy. "What'd you say your name was?"

"Why?" Billy says. "We friends now?"

Pete spits and cocks his head, his bottom lip shining in the headlights. Dry heat burns in Billy's earlobes and cheeks. He wants to stomp his ass into the ditch but wonders what Vonda's been through with him. Best case, it was years of him not showing up, not doing things he said he would.

"I'm just dropping her off," Billy says. "You mind moving your car?"

"Don't you tell me what to do."

Vonda pulls out her phone. "Since I can't talk to you, the sheriff's deputy will."

"Okay," he says. "Fine."

Pete gets in his car and revs the tiny motor a few times. He swerves close as he pulls away, trying to scare them, but Billy and Vonda don't flinch. His taillights disappear around the bend. She apologizes for Pete showing up, his behavior.

"It's okay." He crooked-grins one side of his mouth. "You're not his mama."

At the top of the driveway, she kisses him on the cheek and then the lips. Her mouth tastes like mint. Her touch makes him feverish. She holds his face in her hands and stares into his eyes like she wants to tell him something there isn't enough time to tell. There's never time because you never know what comes next, too fast for you to get out of the way.

She climbs out of the truck and clacks up the steps to the house without looking back.

He wonders, on the ride home, whether she locked the door and the deadbolt. He texts to make sure she does.

Billy walks the square after his Wednesday double-shift, the night air light and fresh after inhaling steam all day over a steel trough. Boys in khakis are scooting girls in skirts along the sidewalks when Hopkins appears in the crowd, ten years older, his face leathery and tan. Faded denim shirt and cowboy boots. Looking good for a man who crossed the yellow line into Billy's car, killing his own daughter.

"Billy," he says, his breath smelling of cheap draft beer. "It's Gerry. I know you remember me."

People bump into Billy's back, mumble excuse me and go around him. "Big night out on the town?"

Hopkins shakes his head. "I've left Sodom behind, Billy. Born again."

"Slumming with the sinners then."

"Where else would Christ walk?"

Billy spits into the storm drain. "I have no earthly idea."

Hopkins frowns. "Got some time for an old man? Let me buy you a coffee."

They find a table in a coffee shop with local art on the wall. A few students study while a group in a corner acts out a scene from a play, one with exaggerated gestures and kneeling people. Billy sits and squares his shoulders. Coming here was a mistake. If he'd gone home after his shift, he might not have seen him again. Another part of him, though, believes this is inevitable, something else to endure and overcome.

Hopkins tells him the judge ruled leniently because he showed such remorse for losing Henrietta. Months later, in jail, a vision appeared.

"I was walking through the desert, so thirsty I felt my throat

                                        Max Hipp

closing up. My lips parched and cracked. Then Christ appeared on the cross, high above me, the sun riding his shoulders. Glory. The biggest brightest star." Hopkins stares up at the can lights as if seeing Christ again. "He came down, his hands cupped like he had water. I opened my mouth like a baby bird. Instead of water, it was blood. I thought I'd choke. But it quenched my thirst."

He pauses like he wants to emphasize the importance of this moment. The coffee is so sugary it's making Billy feel hot and sick, and he decides against drinking more of it.

He woke in his cell again, the pain of losing Henrietta still with him. But Christ's message was clear: He could live on His blood or die in the desert. He told the other inmates. Soon he had a Bible study. When they let him out on good behavior, he promised himself he'd talk about Christ with everyone, spread it to the masses. He felt like Job. And Saul who became Paul. He tells the story slick, like he's said it a hundred times, pausing in the same places for everybody to react the same. It reminds Billy of the televangelists he heard preach as a kid, the loudmouths caught with prostitutes.

One of the actors across the room flops on the floor, loudly feigning death, and Billy realizes he's been afraid of Hopkins since he was a high school senior. This boogeyman divider of before and after who snapped his life in two.

"I've heard this song," he says.

"Everyone knows the tune," Hopkins says, "not everybody sings it."

Billy holds up his hands. Some of the scars are white as a boiled egg. Some have healed darker. Then there's the long surgical one inside his wrist, the pins and steel.

"It fucked me up. But I don't see how you sleep at night."

Hopkins stares at the table. "I deserve a seat in hell and might get it. But there's nothing I can do about the past. All I can handle is what's in front of me. You were just a kid. You wanted to keep playing ball and had a bright future. I took that from you."

With the back of his hand, Billy pushes his coffee to the edge of the table. "You didn't take anything. You just added some things."

"I'm here to tell you I was lost and Jesus took me in." Hopkins glances out the window. "He'll take you, Billy. He'll help with the pain."

"I like the pain," Billy says. "I want to feel it." Saying this to Hopkins is like throwing a fastball for a called strike again, a quick burning down his back muscles.

Hopkins angles his body sideways. "I don't believe anyone wants to carry that around."

"You can believe me because I'm telling you." Billy stands up. "And I don't need life advice from a washed-up old drunk."

Hopkins reaches in his wallet and palms a card onto the table. "It's fine to hate me. I've earned your hate and then some. Just call me if you ever want to talk." He doesn't try to shake Billy's hand before he sidles out into the people, the cars, the lights.

Billy picks up the card. *Do you know Him? I do.* There's a number. He tears it in half and stuffs it in Hopkins' empty cup.

The next weekend, Vonda answers the door in a short dress. Silver and turquoise earrings. The sight of her makes him wish he hadn't started drinking already.

He lets her pick the movie after dinner, a romantic comedy about a man reluctant to marry, still a bachelor in his thirties, who meets the girl of his dreams and wins her by changing his playboy ways. Billy goes to the bathroom twice to pull from his flask before slipping back into the theater. He can't quite focus. But he enjoys Vonda's company

Max Hipp

in the dark, the soft chairs, the air conditioning, the way the movie-makers fill the spaces between scenes with pop songs. Once in a while, he glances at her. She clasps her hands together as she watches. He pictures her in this pose, watching movies as a girl.

They drive to the same shop with the local art and order coffees and slices of red velvet cake and sit at a table by a window facing the street. Cars stop for pedestrians in the crosswalk. A line of slow headlights moves past.

"What'd you think of the movie?" she asks.

"Tell you the truth, I don't like most movies. The characters don't make much sense to me." He remembers again the movie about Paris, Texas and the silent man who wandered the desert for so long, a character he does understand.

She takes another forkful of cake. "People in real life don't really make much sense either." A family walks by the window. She watches him. "So why take a girl to a movie if you don't like them?"

"I saw you." He clasps his hands. "You loved it so much."
She blushes.

He scrapes cake crumbs together and mashes them between the fork tines. "I do like sitting in the dark with the light and sound. It's like old times out on the prairie maybe. When people used to stare at the fire and listen to insects and screech owls." He puts the fork in his mouth, draws it out clean.

She reaches across the table to grab his hand. "It was really nice."

He takes her cold hand and tries to warm it. Her hands are small and soft and all week he's remembered how they felt on his face. He's pulling this off somehow. But his flask is empty.

He says, "I sure could go for a beer."

The band at Itchy's plays hill country blues. It's penny wing night and the place stinks of stale fryer oil. When he orders a beer and a shot for himself, she gives him a long look he hasn't yet seen and says she only wants one beer and goes to stand by herself at a table. Her face is lit by her phone while he waits for the bartender. He takes the shot and drinks half his beer to chase it, orders another beer too. He finishes the first beer and walks over with the two newest ones.

She nods at her phone. "Mom sent me a video." Emily splashes in the bathtub. Seeing the little girl makes him feel like he hasn't screwed this up yet. Maybe he can take Vonda and Emily to a movie one day.

Two songs later, he accidentally finishes his beer before she finishes hers and tries to pretend he hasn't. Then, filled with self-hatred for pretending such things, he announces he's getting another.

She grabs his arm and moves in until his eyes cross and pushes her tongue into his mouth. For a few seconds, her body snaked against his, he forgets every trouble. She keeps her hand on the back of his head as she pulls away. Something trembles in her face, like he's somehow passed her his sorrows. It collapses him inside.

"You win," he says. "No more beers."

She looks down as if something sad is under the table. Her eye whites shimmer like Liquid Paper. "I can't do this again."

"Do what?"

"Can you just take me home, please?"

They pause for a moment and grimly watch a line of frat boys clomp by in dress shoes.

"Look," he says. "I'm sorry. Whatever I did."

"You don't have to say that." She steps toward the door and turns to him. "I just need you to take me home."

He swishes through plowed gravel on the road shoulders, enjoying the wheel shimmying in his grip and the sound of tires losing traction as he swerves and corrects around the curves.

"Maybe we should slow down a little," she says.

He covers his mouth with his fist to burp. This isn't going to get any better and he's not drunk enough to imagine that life is any good. He has this fine woman with him, for instance, and no way to finish the night properly, in bed.

By the time they round the last curve before her driveway, he feels Pete will be there. It's like he conjures the car to block the driveway again just seconds before it appears in the headlights.

Vonda hangs her head. "Unbelievable," she whispers.

"Here we go," Billy says. "Round two. Ding-ding."

When they get out, Pete sets his beer bottle in the middle of the road.

"You stupid motherfucker."

"Hi, Pete," Billy says. "Fancy meeting you here. Real fancy."

"I warned you. Last time was your warning."

"Message received." Billy almost falls over trying to curtsy. "Wanna dance with me?"

Pete points a pistol in his face, black and automatic. "You can dance to this."

"No, no, no!" Vonda screams.

Billy straightens his back and smiles. "Go ahead." How nice it will be to feel something else for a change.

"I will!"

"No, you won't," Vonda says. Her eyes dart at Billy and back to Pete. "Because I'm going with you, baby."

Pete looks at her. "You mean it?"

When Billy grabs the pistol, it fires with a deafening flash. The bullet rips through his side like a hot spike, outrageous pain he hasn't felt since his hands smashed through the dashboard, the plastic and glass snapping like pecans. He snatches the pistol away and cracks Pete in the mouth with it.

Pete goes to his knees in the headlights, his ball cap falling away, his blond hair fine as chicken feathers. Blood and shards of teeth spatter the gravel. He howls.

Vonda presses her knuckles into her temples and looks up at Billy. "Why'd you do that?"

It's so obvious why he did it, he doesn't know what to say. Pete moans into his hands and Vonda begins rubbing his shoulders.

The bullet passed through and left two stinging wounds in his love handle. The pain bulges like an arm punching out of him. Wetness spreads through his shirt and under his belt. It hurts, but not as bad as he imagined a bullet would. And he doesn't want anyone to know. It's *his* pain. He doesn't want to give it to anyone else. Billy groans without meaning to as he tosses the gun in the ditch.

"You didn't have to," Vonda says, her voice breaking. "He wouldn't have done anything." She digs in her purse and unwraps a pack of tissues, puts the whole stack against Pete's sobbing mouth. "You're damn lucky that bullet didn't hit you."

He turns toward the wall of trees rising at the road's edge. Whatever constellations lie beyond, he can't see them. Things get worse no matter what he does.

He picks up Pete's beer bottle, drinks the swill and *thunks* it in the road. Then he turns the truck around.

Soon they're dim red shapes in his taillights.

The blues band is packing up. Twenty minutes until closing, he sits at Itchy's bar and orders rounds of whiskey and beer. He buttoned his coat and got lucky the cigar-smoking doorman didn't notice any blood on his black jeans. The pain subsides into throbbing numbness, a dull soreness that stings when he moves, so he gestures with only his hands each time he orders. College girls parade by in pretty dresses, everyone shouting at a game on TV. Now and again, he catches wafts of his own coppery stench.

Hopkins appears at his elbow and grabs the bar to steady himself.

Billy turns only his head. "How drunk are you, old man?"

He closes one eye, shows Billy his thumb and index finger and the small space between them. He leans close and cups his hand behind his ear. "What do you want to say to me, Billy? I'm here to listen." His voice is strange, almost plaintive.

"That you're a lowdown piece of shit? That you should've died instead of your daughter?" Sweat drops off Billy's ears. "You don't know a goddamn thing about anything."

Hopkins' eyes bug and he spreads his arms wide. "Jesus forgives, Billy. You can sin again and again and he'll forgive you every time. His arms are always open. That's the beauty of the blood." He bows and backs away, a long piss shadow down the front of his jeans.

When he leaves Billy's sight, a girl stands just the other side of where he'd been. Long black hair in her face. Henrietta would be about her age now. The bartender slides a beer bottle, and when her fingers wrap around it, he sees crimson nails. Then the girl goes away so fast, it's like she was never there at all.

"It's time to go!" the bouncer shouts three feet from his face. "The bar is closed!"

Billy lurches to keep his beer, but the bouncer jerks it away. He takes a lazy swing and something tears in his side as he collapses. People lined up to pay their tabs laugh at him.

The bouncer leans over him. "Man, you're making my night longer."

The overhead lights blast on. Everyone squints. The bouncer gets behind and picks Billy up in a half-nelson then lets him slide to the floor. He looks at his hands and arms in disbelief, holds them up for the bartender to see.

"Jesus Christ!" the bartender says.

Billy's coat is stuck to his shirt. He studies the sogginess glued to his hip. Down on the floor, his body is heavy. It's easy to lie back and stare at the lights. He blinks at the ghosts of his eye veins as the bartender tells everyone not to touch the bleeding man. The students spill onto the balcony and down the stairs, hooting and shouting in the street.

Billy wakes up believing his phone is ringing, but his hands are so sticky, he gives up trying to open it. *I didn't like ending the night that way*, he imagines Vonda saying on the phone. *I wanted to thank you. You saved us. And I wanted to say I'm done with Pete.* Billy promises her he'll change his ways. Then she says something he can't hear over the commotion from the stairs.

Two EMTs trudge into the room with a folded-up gurney and soft suitcases. He can't believe how fast they've arrived. They blur on both sides of him and cut his shirt open. The air conditioning burns. The one closest to his face looms barrel-chested like the Christian bodybuilders who came to his junior high and performed feats of strength, ripping phonebooks in half for Jesus.

"Damn," he says. "What did you do?"

"I saved her." Billy struggles to keep his eyes open. "I saved her."

HOW TO PICK UP BEAUTIFUL WOMEN

It's never easy meeting a complete stranger, especially one as beautiful as you, without being properly introduced, but shall we try anyway? (Eagan, 201)

An emo band is blasting onstage and there's this beautiful woman across the bar, wearing a cocktail dress and gold hoop earrings. Her hair is dark red, a different shade from my soon-to-be ex-wife's.

I am an irresistible sex machine.

I go and feed her the line. She just blinks. The guilt and self-hate ball up in my stomach, but I keep it down, away from my face.

"What?" she says.

I say the line again, trimming some of the modifiers because the emo band is now caterwauling. She leans close to my ear.

"Um," she says, rattling my eardrum, "I guess."

I buy us vodka tonics even though she's not quite done with hers.

"Do you like this band?" I scream.

"No!" she shrieks back.

The place is popular, new, and people keep bumping into me.

I can smell everyone's shampoo and cologne.

I say, "After these drinks let's get out of here."

She nods, finishes her first drink, and starts the one I bought for her. Big freckles line her arms and she has fine, soft hairs—nothing like my ex-wife. Patty grows no hair on her arms, is so afraid of the sun and more freckles that she cakes herself with sunblock every day. When I did the laundry her shirts always smelled like the beach.

The beautiful woman and I sit on stools, not really saying anything, not just because of the noise but also because speech might make us think more darkly of ourselves. She looks down, touches the screen of her smart phone. I have a dumb phone. Her phone makes me feel empty and inadequate inside. When she goes to the bathroom, I realize I haven't even asked her name.

The band crashes and bashes through their loudest songs for the finale. The strobes flash and people up front lose themselves in the spectacle, but back here we are missing the point of it all.

The beautiful no-name woman doesn't return. The band throws guitar picks and drumsticks at the crowd. I finish our drinks.

Hi, a beautiful woman like you should have a great evening, give me a chance to let that happen. May I join you in a drink? (Ibid.)

In a drink. Why *in* a drink? I sit at the bar and can't get it out of my skull. It's as if I'm asking the beautiful woman to step with me into a Jacuzzi-sized martini glass. John Eagan, author of *How to Pick Up Beautiful Women*, puts B.A. after his name on the cover of his book. I have an M.A. and teach composition at Southeastern State Community College. The grammar in Eagan's pickup line is wrong, wrong like my life.

After a few vodka tonics, two blonds and a brunette walk in

and take a booth. I look around and a couple guys, one in a plaid
sport coat and the other swaying drunkenly on a stool, instantly
bird-dog these ladies. I decide to act. According to Harville
Hendrix, Ph.D., author of *Keeping the Love You Find*, I must work
on my *action*. I've got *thought* and *feeling* down. It's *sensing* and
action I need to work on, so I'm across that room like a spider
monkey on angel dust.

According to Eagan, when there are several women, you must
buy them all drinks. It costs, but so does life. You'll lose more
money than drink money in your life, especially on something like
a divorce.

I deliver the first sentence of the line. Then I say, "May I join
you *for* a drink?"

They look at each other and laugh. I've got a new black dress
shirt tucked into my jeans. Chest poked out, shined leather shoes. I
know I look good. I *am* a sex machine.

"Are you buying?" asks the one I want, her lips shiny with
gloss, her pushup bra and top displaying cleavage. Like the bras
Patty bought from Victoria's Secret, the ones that could not help us.

"Of course," I say.

They giggle in unison.

"Sit," she says, and offers her hand. Her name is Marley. "My
mom liked reggae," she says. "A lot."

Marley's hair springs from her scalp in long, tight braids.
She's a nurse at the children's hospital and also an actress. In fact,
she's acting in a few plays across town. She aims her body at me
when she speaks. It's a good night to be alive, in the company of
beautiful women.

Her blond friends, Sidney and Keeley, go sit at the bar where
other men buy them drinks.

"You have great friends," I say. "That says a lot about you."

"So where are your friends?"

I consider this. "I'm losing most of them in the divorce."

Then I have to do a lot of talking. I talk about the separation and Patty sleeping with her boss. I don't talk about the heartbreak and the loneliness. That pain belongs to me alone and, besides, I want to have a good time. Marley's body language never closes up. She listens. Maybe there's hope. Maybe there's life after losing so much.

Pretty soon her friends want to go. It's late. They work early in the morning. There's a long drive home. There are a million reasons to say goodbye to the night.

"Give me your number."

"No," she says. "Give me yours." As she puts my number in her phone, I ask her why. "I don't date married men," she says. "But we can be friends."

The wind gushes out of my lungs. I hang in there, though, smile on face, showing the teeth.

We shake hands goodnight. In that dress, from behind, honest to god, she looks like a violin, a Stradivarius, a work of art. Another beautiful woman walks out of my life.

I'm not trying to be rude or impolite, or invade your space in any way. I just wanted to know if a lovely girl like you can use some pleasant company? (Ibid.)

I have fifteen-minute conferences with students about their personal narratives. The author of the narrative about a highway patrolman carrying nunchuks walks in. She has curves I've never seen in class because, until now, they've been hidden beneath thigh-length t-shirts. She's made up her face and is wearing a low-cut top. I realize she's closer in age to my ancient thirty years than she is to her fellow freshmen.

I smell a setup.

But wait!

Maybe she's my *Imago*, Dr. Harville Hendrix's word for my romantic match. Maybe she can help me resolve conflicts with my parents and how they fell apart. Maybe it's only incidental that she's my student and I'm her instructor. More mysterious things have happened in the universe, have they not?

I look at her paper and ask about the nunchuks. She giggles and flushes red. "I have to be honest," she says. "I made that up." She leans forward so I can look at the goods. I don't. Or at least I'm not obvious about it.

"Well," I say, "it's good writing, but I don't believe it."

"You don't think the nunchuks add tension?" She pulls out her notebook, licks her fingers and starts turning pages, red nails on white paper. "Because, Mr. Little, you told us last week that every narrative needs tension."

I go into my lecture voice and tell her it is the right detail in the right place, blah, blah, blah, that makes a good narrative. While I talk, she unsheathes a lollipop and wraps her lips around it, pushes and turns it against her tongue. In this moment, I realize I have been visiting too many porn sites and my sex drive is off the charts. Those images burn into the crevices of your brain, by the way. At the end of my screed I'm almost babbling, but she isn't listening anyway.

"And that's why *nunchuks* has to go," I say.

She replies, "I'll do whatever you want, Mr. Little." She crunches down on the red lollipop.

I realize she's said my line to me with her eyes and body and I'm the one being picked up. This beautiful woman knows a sex machine when she sees one. She understands that I'm worthy of love.

Hi, I just wanted to tell you that what you are wearing looks stunning on you. May I join you? (Ibid.)

This beautiful woman is at the coffee shop, wearing a tank top and jeans, nothing I would call stunning. She's got big green eyes, nothing like Patty's brown ones. At this crucial moment, Patty calls me. We're trying to be friends, but I no longer like her.

"Will, we need to talk about everything," she says.

"I don't want to talk about everything," I say. "Life is short."

"Connie says you're out every night going to bars. Do you have any idea how sad that is?"

Constance is Patty's best friend who also lurks at the law firm. Phil Grill's law firm. Grill and Sprinkle, Attorneys at Law. Those are *action* names. My last name is Little, an overused adjective. I wrack my brain but don't remember seeing Constance anywhere. Perhaps it's because she's not a beautiful woman.

I say to Patty, "Do you know how sad it is for a forty-year-old born-again virgin to go to bars and be up in my business?"

"Don't make fun of Connie," she says. "She's only looking out for you."

Blood rushes to my face. I picture Patty sprawled on Phil Grill's desk, white garters on her thighs, though, to my knowledge, she's never worn such undergarments.

"Was she looking out for me when I would call for you? Was she looking out for me when she would lie and say you were in a meeting?"

Silence.

"You're changing the subject," she says.

I hang up. She calls back. I press *reject* and erase the voicemail without listening to it.

The woman with the big green eyes is still waiting. I hold the words of the pickup line in my mouth, tapping them against my teeth. When I begin to move, a man in overalls slips into her booth and grabs her hand.

Stunning.

I was intrigued by your beauty and grace, and I just couldn't keep myself from coming over. May I join you in a drink? (Eagan, 202)

Nunchuks and I schedule a special midnight study session, with drinks.

She gets dressed and we shake hands like it's business. She opens my office door to go.

"Listen," she says, "I'm going to be out of town for the rest of the semester. Do you think you could use your knack for detail and specificity to imagine my future papers into existence? I'd appreciate it."

I look out the window. Not even the stars can watch this.

"Oh," she says, smacking the back pocket of her jeans for emphasis, "and it's A for ass."

Her heels snap down the long empty hallway.

Hi, I've seen that king [sic] of dress on other women, but none of them looked as great as you do in it. Do you mind if I join you? (Ibid.)

A typo? Are you kidding me? These are the most important words of a three-hundred-page book, and he decides to misspell one of them. I begin to wonder if I've taught Eagan, if he's been in one of my composition classes, writing *it's* for *its*, *then* for *than*, *effect* for *affect*, *accept* for *except*, *lose* for *loose*, *quite* for *quiet*, and *there* for *their* and *they're*.

I go to the club in search of the king of dress. She is nowhere. My imagination is too blank to conjure her. My hand picks a bottle of Wild Turkey from behind the bar. I stand in the alley with it before great darkness descends and wipes my memory for a few hours.

Next thing, cars line the curbs along both sides of the street. In the blinding porchlight, silhouettes hold Solo cups. People talk loudly in drunken deafness and stare at me as I stumble up the sidewalk. I don't recognize any of the shadowed faces but keep moving toward the front door as if I have some purpose.

A clutch of drunks on soiled couches in the living room, tapestries on the walls and sheets over the windows, CDs and DVDs spread on the floor beneath the TV like humdrum offerings. I find the keg in the kitchen where a tall drunk kid in a baseball cap offers me a yellow cup from a stack. He pumps the tap and ice water rattles in the garbage can as I aim the spout.

I kick aside some trash and go out onto the back porch where a bare bulb illuminates gray decking and a few feet of grass beyond it. There is nothing out here but squirrels and birds huddling in the live oaks. The back door opens and out comes a powerfully built kid with another bottle of whiskey. He has on a tight undershirt and jeans, no shoes. Someone has smeared lipstick on his face. He passes me the bottle without speaking. I take it, unscrew, drink, re-screw, and pass it back.

He nods. "What's your name?"

I've been reading Shakespeare. "Falstaff," I say.

He laughs and passes me the bottle again. "Whatever."

When I pass it back he sets it on the rail and pulls a smart phone from his pocket. A pale, blue light shines on his face. It's an expensive one, with internet and everything imaginable. He can use it to check out of life whenever it bores him. Patty scrolling through sexts and emails from Phil Grill, big smile on her face. Scrolling and smiling, treacherous and banal.

In the light, his jawline is illuminated. My first instinct was *thinking*, but I'm sure this is the time for *action*. He is too preoccupied to see me rear back and take aim. I miss his face completely, fall and bang my head down the steps into the yard, my feet catching at the top, soles skyward. I remain conscious long enough to hear the entire house party come to the rail and laugh.

As I was standing there, I noticed how beautiful you were. I thought perhaps we could spend our time more agreeable together. May I join you? (Ibid.)

Were instead of *are*, as if beauty fades with time, which is not what you want a beautiful woman to think about when you are trying to enter her life. You don't want her thinking about death the way you do. That's no way to find your *Imago*.

Ice in a ziplock bag against my swollen head. My skull isn't broken, but an enormous broken-blood-vessel bruise at the temple lopsides my face. The pain of it almost makes me forget my hangover. As it loops in my head, Eagan's *our time more agreeable* sounds like poetry.

The house smells like last night's chicken bucket. I click an email from the chair of my department. It seems Nunchuks has been arrested for drug-running in El Paso, violating her parole. Her parents are furious. The chair would like me to come in immediately to explain how Nunchuks has maintained her stellar average from such geographical distance.

I get dressed and make myself presentable if *presentable* means looking less like a corpse. I smile in the mirror. Somehow all teeth are still present.

The sun beats through my sunglasses. I manage to get out of the car, through the parking lot, and into the building without vomiting. The chair's office door is wide open. Her assistant waves me in like an air-traffic controller.

"William," the chair says, getting up, her face clouding with concern. "Are you under the weather?"

She's wearing a cream-colored blouse and rouge on her cheeks. For a split second, I consider my *Imago* and how perhaps I've been looking at this meeting all wrong. Maybe this is the time for pickup lines. I try my own.

"I'm just fine, Ruth. You're looking lovely today."

She nods and sits, so I do the same.

"I know you've been going through some trouble lately. Of course, I heard about Patty. But this is something else altogether."

She tells me Nunchuks' father is a big donor and that the provost has spoken and now is the time is for decisive *action*. My contract won't be renewed. I'll be relieved of my classes and have to adjunct elsewhere. Everyone is very sorry for these unfortunate circumstances.

I zone out, thinking about life and my place in it. There's a pause and I realize she's expecting me to respond.

I say, "I thought we might spend our time more agreeable."

I've never really said this to anyone before, but I just felt I had to tell you—you're the most beautiful woman I've ever seen. (Ibid.)

I should stay home, but there's this voice inside saying whatever will fix my life is not at my house. The fix isn't inside me, either. It's out there, running through magical fields with the beautiful women.

Down by the beach there's an old bar where tourists flock for the holiest of Gulf Coast holidays, Spring Break. Luckily, it's the offseason and there's time and space to think. I go out looking for the most beautiful woman I've ever seen. I don't want to lie, so she

                                    Max Hipp

at least has to be in the ballpark of the most beautiful woman I've ever seen. Maybe just in the same zip code.

The place serves crab. There's a constant fishy odor and the reek of beer-soaked floorboards. The one woman in the bar is wearing a strapless linen dress with turquoise bikini straps on her browned shoulders. I sit down next to her and see that her face is lined from decades spent sunning. But, yes, it's quite possible that twenty years ago she would've been the most beautiful woman I have ever seen.

For a moment, I don't think I can go through with this but I snap out of it. This is what single people do: they deliver the lines. I give it to her and she smiles, she absolutely beams at me. I'm instantly sorry that I have stolen the line from Casanova, B.A. and that I couldn't make her smile by my own wit.

Turns out she is a good person, with ideas, a heart, and a mind of her own. On her smart phone, she shows me pictures of her children and it doesn't make me feel inadequate. They are in college, smiling, happy. She tells me that their father is no longer with us. I don't pry. Death is not the path to sex.

I tell her about my ex and how she wronged me. I tell her I'm still doing the job I lost. I talk about how I've been going to the gym to stay sane and get my body together. I'm not fit, just gaunt with stringy muscles, but I offer my knobby biceps to feel, my budding, angular pecs.

"Wow!" she says, genuinely impressed. "So strong! So full of life!"

After laying hands on me, she doesn't take them off again. She squeezes my knee when she's telling a story. She touches my shoulder when she laughs. It almost creeps me out, but I understand she's taking *action*.

When we leave the crab place we are hot for each other in the alley. Our hands are wandering, searching for the parts that will stave off the loneliness. Her place is close, on the beach, but we drive my car to get there faster. Maybe all this work, this devotion to and study of beautiful women will finally pay off. Someone will appreciate and validate who and what I am. I am more than an ex-composition instructor. I am a sex machine.

Inside her condo the first thing I notice is the mechanical hiss. She tries to kiss and moan over it. She is telling me how incredible I am, how special and kind. She won't flip on lights and is trying to pull me down the hall. But I feel the switch digging into my shoulder blade and flick it. There, in the dining room, is her husband, a husk of a man hooked to tubes, tanks, and a breathing machine. He is preserved by the respirator, yet lifeless as a dining room table.

She sees the look of horror on my face. Her mouth starts shaping words a few seconds before anything comes out.

"Don't go," she says.

"I really should," I say.

"No, you shouldn't." Her eyes are wide and electric with longing. "It's okay. Stay here with me."

The hissing fills the space between us. We try to hold our breaths but the machine breathes for both of us. There are people lonelier than we are. There are lives more ragged and *actions* more desperate than anything Harville Hendrix could imagine. There's no pickup line for this.

She places my hand over her heart. She holds it there, almost trembling.

Lonesome is a world.

DEATH MAY BE YOUR SANTA CLAUS

MICA

When you think about killing someone so long, scenarios run through your head. In the trailer park in Jacksonville, I'd stare at the ceiling mildew that sang like Alvin and the Chipmunks and see Redgrove beaten until his face swelled like a pumpkin. I saw his strangled body bound and gagged the way he'd left Susanne. Like a piece of road trash.

They let him out of Raiford. I knew he'd go to his father's office in the morning to pretend to work. I laid in the woods and watched him smoke on his porch.

In the end I did the obvious thing. I aimed my .22 when he opened the car door and let the blood out of his head for him. He stared through me—I thought he hated me the way I hated him—but it was only dying. I'd pictured his death so many times, I thought I'd feel one way or the other.

I didn't feel any way at all.

BRIGGS

Mica had his hands in his pockets, his too-big t-shirt blowing against his ribs. What was left of his hair whipped blond flares around his face. He waved like he was wiping steam off a mirror. He'd grown skinnier since Redgrove killed Susanne and practically got away with it.

I got out and yelled against the wind, "You look about half dead."

He said, "You look about the same."

We walked the beach and smelled the brine and dead fish. People would leave guts for the gulls, but gulls wanted potato chips and garbage.

We neared the old pier, stanchions rising like rotted, gray teeth from a giant jaw. Where the rocks stretched into the water marked the border we never crossed as kids.

They'd cut Redgrove loose and I didn't want to bring it up. But if the man who killed my wife had got out early for good behavior, I'd talk about it. I'd make a stink all over town.

He pulled a ciggie-boo from his breast pocket and backed into the wind to cup the flame.

"How about one for old Briggs?"

He started another from the tip and passed it. The smoke gave me a burst of heat in the cold wind off the Atlantic.

"Thought you quit."

"Old friends," I said, "bring back old ways."

He stared at the breakers and the pale sky stretched to the other side of the world. Sunken wrecks out there, rumors of treasure and weighted bodies.

"I got trouble," he said.

"I know that bastard's loose and out breathing free air. But you're still breathing too. Don't lose sight of that."

He stared at the sand. His eyelids puckered around the whites.

"Redgrove isn't breathing anymore." He dropped the butt and heeled it.

MICA

I'd thought so much in Jacksonville about revenge and wrongdoing, I remembered every bad thing ever done to me. I needed someplace to hole up and knew about Briggs' hunting cabin in the boonies. Briggs and Susanne had spent some nights together the first time she and I had broken up. I thought Briggs and me were good once, but now I wasn't sure. I followed his car and hoped him putting me up might make it right.

The cabin was living space and kitchen. A wood-burning stove. No screens on the windows, no fans. The stagnant air smelled of rot, the way my trailer always did when I got home from a shift at Becker's Crab Shack.

"Home sweet." Briggs flashed teeth. He'd taken the news of me killing Redgrove like a champ. He folded out the couch and brushed mouse turds off the mattress. He brought musty sheets from the closet and made the bed. His fat ass leaned all over it.

"I appreciate it," I said.

"Hey pal, anything I can do." He went in the kitchen, his steps like dull thunder on the plywood, and came back with a dusty bottle of Kentucky Tavern and two sippy cups with Scrooge McDuck on the side. "This feels like the right time to crack her open."

His mouth grinned. His eyes didn't.

That hot box made me think of Susanne, the way she'd punch me in the gut to wake me sometimes, how I'd gasp, angry, until I saw the love in her eyes. My wild one. I tried to remember the name of that Mott the Hoople song that made her dance so sexy. I still didn't know how Redgrove could've looked into her and done

what he did. It occurred to me maybe he hadn't done it alone.
I pictured Briggs and Susanne, Briggs and Redgrove, everybody
fucking each other and fucking each other over.

My mind snapped on the idea. Briggs had been part of her
death all along, hiding in plain sight. It felt like something I'd
known, something inevitable.

Briggs set a sippy cup in front of me and raised his to eye-level.

"To friends," he said.

BRIGGS

The next morning, I scanned the internet for any mention of
Redgrove's body. I went to the bathroom at the hardware store and
stared at the toilet while my stomach heaved up nothing. It finally
surfaced on WJXT news: St. Augustine Businessman Found Slain.

I'd felt for Mica when Redgrove went away for manslaughter
instead of murder. Defense said Susanne was into rough sex, that
her death was a game they played when they took MDA and whatever else. Ball gags and zip ties. Hell, she scared me, that's why we
were just friends. But Mica must've felt awful in that courtroom.
What would it be like to have your murdered wife disgraced in the
public record? I thought about the roller coaster of justice, how it
tips upside down, blows your hat off and dumps change from your
pockets. Everything you thought was yours falls into the weeds.

I sat behind the counter at Ace, checking people out, remem-
bering verses. Cain said to God, "Am I my brother's keeper?" I
wasn't Cain, I was Abel. In the story you were either murdered or
the murderer. The golden rule said, Do unto others as you would
have them do unto you. I'd taken Mica in, my brother's keeper, the
role Cain scorned before God.

I took off work, went home and sat in the bathtub, pulled the

                                                  Max Hipp

Bugs Bunny shower curtain closed. Junior was working a double at Dairy Queen. Maybelline would be home any minute.

Redgrove had screwed Susanne behind Mica's back. Since everyone in town knew, I figured he knew too. You think he's okay with it, like they've got some arrangement. Part of him must've known because he never asked, "Why didn't anyone tell me?" but maybe her being manslaughtered made him overlook that part. Or maybe he never could see her straight. The one you love can tear your heart out, drop a cigarette butt down the pipes, and you'll say, "For me?" and grin.

Maybelline came home from the clinic in her scrubs. She held her keys as I laid out Mica murdering Redgrove with my aiding and abetting like a stringer of rotten fish. She slumped in the kitchen and lit a Parliament without looking at it, or me.

"I'm going to ask you again like I did when this shitstorm plowed through the first time." She blew smoke up into her bangs. "Is there anything you won't do just cause you've known these people your whole life?" When I didn't answer, she said, "He could murder all of us. Did you think about that?"

She was Adam's rib, I knew, but Adam's rib was often smarter than me. It was enough for her to toss these questions in the air. Even when she went in the bathroom and ran water, I still heard her words.

"He could murder us," I said to the backyard.

The sunset pinkened the clouds. Planes chemtrailed silently overhead.

MICA

In one corner of the shack, Briggs had pinned relics from his college dorm: a dusty dartboard and a poster of a woman from the nose down, arms covering her nipples, with the caption, "Man cannot live on beer alone." The darts wouldn't fly right and the cork in the board was too dried out to catch them. I threw at the woman, got one in her neck.

Out behind the cabin I found a stream. I knelt in the sand with a cigarette hung from my lip and watched the riffles and water bugs. Water always made me think of times at the beaches, under the piers, in the car at night with the windows down, wind wilding her hair while the surf pounded. Water over two thirds of the Earth and Susanne forever in hard ground. We'd get high and listen to records if she were here. We'd be free.

BRIGGS

Friday morning, she packed and left for her mother's. Junior stayed at a friend's house. "If I don't go tonight," I told her, "he'll know something's up."

I hefted her bag into the trunk and she almost slammed my hand in it.

"The only move here is to call the police." She stared at me over the Toyota roof and said, "Briggs, I can't take much more."

She drove off and left me with feelings I didn't enjoy.

I sat on the porch with one of her ciggie-boos and watched Mr. Fante weedwack his monkey grass. I might've been my brother's keeper, but Mica was Cain. Mica was the brother-killer and Redgrove the sister-killer, though the Bible didn't have much to say about sisters that I could recall. We'd been four, then three. Now two.

Cops always made things worse. They gave me DUIs. They hauled my father in for fighting our neighbor, Mr. Argyle, who set our electrical box on fire to burn an ant bed, the last straw for my

Max Hipp

old man. He punched Argyle in the nose for not agreeing to pay for
the VCR his stunt had shorted out. Whenever I saw police cruisers,
I pictured my old man's bald head and yellow eyes glaring from the
back seat.

I felt obliged to Maybelline *and* to Mica. Not Mica the killer
but the kid who sweated out football practice with me. I didn't
think that kid could kill me.

Then it came to me. He couldn't try anything if I knocked him
out. He'd go to sleep peacefully, which would give me more time
to think about calling the cops on him. It would give me time to
think about being his Judas.

I went to May's side of the medicine cabinet and ground up a
bunch of her sleepers. He wouldn't taste it in burgers, I'd see to it.

MICA

Briggs' crimson Buick roared up the dirt road on Friday evening.
I tucked the pistol under my shirt. His face looked agreeable and
dumb as a stump. He popped the trunk to Cheetos, Cokes, white
bread, American cheese, sliced turkey, milk, Cap'n Crunch, a bag
of potatoes, and a watermelon. He'd brought premade burgers and
a little grill.

"I really appreciate it, Briggsy." I slapped his shoulder and
squeezed. For a man who had helped murder Susanne, he sure was
nice. I wondered if I could tie him down and shoot one tooth out
of his mouth at a time, how long he'd live if I did.

We got everything lit and eaten and sat drinking Kentucky
Tavern under the stars, orange firelight in our faces. I pulled from
my sippy cup and tried to picture Susanne sitting on Briggs' lap. A
mermaid fucking a whale.

"You've done so much for me, buddy," I said. "I don't know

how to repay you."

The smile came back, a crack across Humpty Dumpty's face. "Everything's going to be all right," he said.

"Nothing's ever all right with Susanne gone." In the shadow in my lap, I fingered the pistol handle's sharp grooves.

"It's been a rough road, man." His face spread wider in the firelight, panoramic, like sky over a sea. "But things will turn around."

"Why?" My mouth thickened. It took a lot to get the one word out.

"Because they have to."

I felt warm and jittery like I floated in a hot tub with butterflies on me, wild horses kicking dirt on a plateau in perpetual twilight. Sleep lay on top of me, hugged close and too hard, unnatural. I shook myself and realized my mouth was open with drool down my chin.

I stood from the camp chair, tried to focus on Briggs as he got up and backed away. I pulled the pistol and shot the ground as it rose to meet me.

BRIGGS

He ate more of the dosed ones than I'd figured. He weighed less than Maybelline.

"I thought I was low before," he said, his mouth full of meat, "but I've never been lower than now."

Terrified as I was, I felt for him. He was that skinny kid on a bike with mud sprayed up the back of his shirt. The one his father resented for existing. He'd tell Mica in front of me, "You're a waste of my retirement money."

He hit the ground hard when he tried to shoot me. Meanness flaring in his eyes before he passed out.

Maybe I was Cain too. Cain killing Cain. Maybe the Abels were driven from the Earth long ago and everyone in the world now was Cain.

MICA

I must've sleep-crawled into the woods. I woke with ants all over me and cops swarming the cabin with shotguns. They brought every car they weren't washing at the carwash across from the tote-some on Ponce de Leon. I spotted a guy I went to high school with and remembered how rumors spread in St. Augustine like chlamydia.

I flipped a quarter. It flashed silver into the weeds.

My shirt felt hot. I took it off and walked back to the stream. Before I'd passed out, I'd seen Briggs run for his car like on a blurry TV. He'd got me before I could get him. It occurred to me maybe I wasn't as smart as I thought. If I couldn't get him to pay for Susanne, I was stuck. I thought of that palm reader who said, "Your life is filled with hurt."

I took off everything, put the pistol on the pile, and let the cold stream wash my ankles, shins, knees. I splashed my face and squatted. A breeze blew when you got low, only your head above water.

That's when she walked downstream to meet me, her hair dyed orange like when we first met. She wore the scratchy dress with the colorful stitching she'd brought back from Taos.

"Are you going to live in the creek now?"

Her voice made me smile. "Yes, ma'am."

She clasped hands above her head and stood on one leg. No water dropped from her. "Are we about done here, sexy?"

"Depends. You good?"

She whistled low, shook her head and grinned. I rocked back, let the water close over my face. She was gone when I came up.

I forgot to ask the name of that damn Mott the Hoople song.

BRIGGS

I watched TV and avoided windows and felt Mica like a tornado pressure-drop even when I knew he was still passed out in the woods. They say the Lord won't give more than you can handle. But he'll find your limits.

At five I went to the only 7-Eleven with a payphone and left an anonymous tip that the murderer of Lawrence Redgrove was lodged at a secluded hunting cabin. I gave the address and hung up and felt awful.

Back in my driveway, I asked Jesus what to do. If I turned myself in, they might go lenient. Or I could wait for the call and say, "I had no earthly idea, officer, my old friend was at my hunting cabin." Then I thought about the roller coaster of justice and how it snakes into the lake upside down and waterboards you. Cops push you into cruisers, make you perp-walk for cameras.

I noticed the long weedy grass and got hold of myself. I was Donald Briggs and this was my home the cops couldn't take.

I got the mower from the shed.

MICA

I climbed the bank and dripped. The pants stuck to my wet legs. I left the shoes and socks, put the pistol in my waistband. Through the trees I saw more blue lights.

In Jacksonville, there'd been a waitress who needed me. She sidled up to tables, rubbed her lower back. If I'd been a different man, I'd still be there to catch her eye from a booth or a lawn chair, to teach her boys to fish and work splinters out of their

Max Hipp

fingers with pocketknives. That's the kind of man who lets go before he gets swallowed.

I put on my shirt when I got close to the cops. An SUV pulled up, the K9 unit.

The quarter I'd flipped glinted at me from the brush. I put my hand over it, felt the ridges, closed my fist.

Heads was suicide, tails suicide by cop.

BRIGGS

I flopped on the couch, cut grass in my leg hairs, watched people play baseball hundreds of miles away. I pictured cops trying to cram an inflatable, giant Mica into a paddy wagon. I knew he'd never go to jail like I knew how Bible pages flitted against my thumb. The consequences of what I'd done twisted me up.

I set my Bible on my chest and laid down to nap.

In the dream, my fingers moved like caterpillar legs. Cop Jesus interrogated me. I told him, "I didn't know he'd killed anybody when I offered the hunting camp! I thought he needed time to think!" Then it wasn't Jesus but Maybelline as my torture cop. "I've never made you happy," I told her, "I don't think it's in me." She glared like I was on a cruise ship headed to Maui and hadn't invited her.

The landline woke me. I sat up, startled, couldn't answer. Jesus wouldn't move my feet.

MICA

I leaned against the tree and remembered the name of her song. It was "Death May Be Your Santa Claus," off *Brain Capers*.

One of the cop cars started blaring it over the loudspeaker. Susanne climbed out in a blue uniform and frisbeed her hat over the cabin. She rolled on the hood, stood and snaked her hips to the music, way more alive than any of us.

When Mott the Hoople hit the groove in the bridge, I felt it in my thighs. The cops started dancing along. They swung around in bulletproof vests and sunglasses, synchronized, like MTV in the '80s.

I cocked the hammer and walked into the sunshine. In that moment, with Susanne on the cop car, the heavens rang with beauty. Pain was almost a stranger.

Max Hipp

CLIFF BURTON RULES

'm hitting the bong on the roof when Cliff Burton, the undead soul of Metallica, leaps down from the trees. Gray cowboy hat with black felt ribbon, flannel shirt with the sleeves cut off, wavy auburn hair to his nipple pockets, bullet belt, bellbottoms. Cliff from 1986, the year of black ice and his bus-wreck death. I've got Cliff's skull ring on my bird finger, the one Ziggler swore he flung at a concert in '85 and sold me for thirty bucks. This must be how I've summoned him to my roof from the astral plane.

"I heard about you, man," he says.

I cough up a cloud. "Me?"

"Still shredding?"

"It's all I do."

"Shit, motherfucker." He closes one nostril and slugs a snot rocket onto the shingles. "You're on your way."

A shooting star flares green over our cul-de-sac and skips my brain like a record. I wonder how far shooting stars are visible, whether Wayne, my dad, can see them wherever he is. Mom says he's probably chasing skirts.

Cliff disappears. It's still better than Jesus revisiting.

I climb in my bedroom window, refasten the screen, turn on my tiny no-name trash amp as loud as possible because Mom and

Rick are out dancing to Vanilla Ice and Digital Underground. I've learned every riff on the first four albums and as many of Kirk Hammett's licks as I can. I don't care if Nirvana has killed guitar shredder solos and grunge is calling the shots—what's dead will live through me.

I blow through the first half of "One" but have to start over because the outro solo is fucking hard. I dream of my thrash band, the albums we'll make, our drummer double-kicking at two hundred forty beats per minute. A family of road warriors who ride tour buses and drink suitcases of beer together.

I stare at the poster over my bed of Metallica, sweaty and shirtless in jeans after some coliseum show. I swear Cliff winks.

My Taco Hell uniform is purple hat, purple shirt tucked into navy pants, scratchy like my polyester Little League uniform was, everything too big.

It's my second week and Pam, the manager, gets friendlier every shift. "Hey, cute Sammy." She wolf-whistles. She's thick-hipped, with fake eyelashes and baby pink lipstick, and tall, two of me easy. I smile and say hello. She slurps me with her eyes and slips into the manager office. It's the first time I've considered myself eye-fuckable.

"Dang, white boy." Marlon's by the steam troughs with the rectangular meat scoop, his face like he's seen a ghost, and the ghost is me. "I think she wants you in her Polaroid collection. For real." Marlon is in college, paying his way with this job. He scissors a bag of frozen meat and dumps it in the trough. It mixes with the old and voila: edible.

When shift boredom sets in I remember the Peavey TNT 150 I'm going to buy once I save enough. A bass amp with a fifteen-inch speaker I'm going to play guitar through. It's sitting at

Bill Boy's EZ Pawn. If I run my DOD pedal through it, I can get James Hetfield's *chugga-chugga* sound. The law says fifteen isn't old enough to work much per week, which means at $4.25 an hour it might take a year.

"Uh-oh," Marlon says, looking at his screen. "They fucking us now. *LORETTA!*" he screams. "*DON'T DO THIS SHIT TO ME!*"

Loretta peeks around the corner, purple lipstick, dimples, drive-thru headset. "I know you ain't trying to tell me what to do." She points at Marlon with a purple fingernail and disappears around the corner. It's Tuesday, so Loretta smells like cotton candy. On Thursday she'll smell like maple syrup.

Marlon scoops meat into taco shells, wraps burritos in Taco Hell wax paper and slides them two at a time down the line where I pull handfuls of lettuce, cheese, and onions out of plastic bins and squeeze guacamole and sour cream from enormous caulk guns. I pop MexiMelts and Mexican Pizzas in the hissing steamer until it beeps.

I box up tacos and Loretta smiles when I hand her the bags. When she bends through the drive-thru window, it should make me dream, yet I feel only metal.

Loretta wants Marlon, Marlon wants himself, Pam wants me, and I want world domination.

Mom and Rick keep discovering old CD singles at Camelot Music. Technotronic, Bel Biv Devoe, Young MC, Tone Loc. I don't know where they learn it, but they Roger Rabbit, Hammertime, pop and lock, dirty dance, forbidden dance. On Thursday I come home from Taco Hell and they're at it, pink and breathless.

"Hey, there, big man!" Rick and I high-five. "Down low!" I reach out but he whips his hand back, frisks his wavy mullet. "Too slow!" he howls.

"Rick," Mom says, "don't tease him!" But she likes the way he teases me. Teasing me is the whole point.

"I tell you what, Sammy, you're a good kid. I'm telling you, man. You're learning the value of a hard day's work. That's gonna serve you well, bud. Take a look at me! I don't go nowhere or look at nothing for less than eighty-five bucks." He whistles high then low. "Now you think about what eighty-five bucks would buy you, my man. And sometimes I get paid eighty-five bucks just to come out and look at a pipe and say, *NOPE!*" He slaps his knee and cackles like it's the funniest thing in the world.

Mom shakes her head. "Rick, you are too much." She grins at me, then rests her eyes on Rick again. When I see her love for him, I hate.

Hate reminds me we're "Disposable Heroes" for the "Master of Puppets" and his "Leper Messiah." It'll go like this: learn unholy riffs, write my own, and start the band, conquer Monsters of Rock, cover the earth with shrapnel and fire.

I go to my room and kneel before my guitar case to unleash the flying V. I practice scales for hours, write riffs using the devil's triad, the Phrygian mode, the harmonic minor. Then I open my lyric book and hiss tales of holy wars and decapitation.

That night I blast away Rick's music and the *swish* of the MexiMelt steamer with Slayer on my Walkman. Slayer is headbanging among the pyramids at Giza. A feeling of peace washes over me. Daddy Wayne plows through the world and forgets I exist, but through metal I am cleansed and tempered.

Harold's house backs up to a pasture where we hunt with flashlights to find shrooms protruding like alien tongues from pancaked piles of cow shit. We stuff them in brown paper bags and twist the tops closed. Mushrooms in the bag are money in the thrill bank.

Afterward we suck Harold's one-hitter and blow smoke into a toilet paper tube stuffed with fabric softener until his room smells Downy fresh. His mom never bothers us. His dad is away on business five nights a week. Harold coughs and passes the smell-silencer and one-hitter along. He's got photos of Morbid Angel, Crowbar, and Obituary ripped from magazines on his walls. Black light posters of a clown, a devil with steer horns, a wizard's tower. If I had those in my room, Rick would ask questions. He acts cool around Mom, sure, but if his country ass heard one Deicide album he'd go full satanic panic and whisk me off to dumb people talking about Jesus.

We watch *Headbangers Ball* and pray for something heavy, wade through grunge until new Metallica comes on, the awful Metallica. When "Enter Sandman" became an MTV smash, the Metallica we loved crashed their helicopter into Cocaine Mountain.

It bums us out.

We turn it off, slip *Cliff 'Em All* in the VCR and watch young Metallica buy convenience store beers and goof with reporters again. They could be my brothers, if Mom and Wayne had stayed together long enough to have any kids but me. They could've made a whole band for me to front if Wayne hadn't stepped out. Mom always calls it *stepping out*, like leaving your family is like exiting a shower stall.

On the VHS tape, Metallica slays at Day on the Green in San Francisco, a town that might as well be the Lost City of Atlantis to us Mississippi metalheads.

"Taco Hell is my gateway to the tower of metal," I say, high enough to be struck by truth. "If you want blood, you must sacrifice."

Harold stares at the popcorn ceiling. "It's a good lyric." I wish Harold could play an instrument but he's going to be a doctor—useless.

I pull a spiral notebook out of Harold's bookbag and start writing.

Onscreen Cliff Burton headbangs a windmill of hair at the crowd. His distorted wah-wah bass churns them into a mosh pit. He wears a denim jacket and faded bell-bottoms. He's twenty-one, twenty-two. Like every rock star who died young, he looks beamed from another planet.

The next Tuesday night, a stomach bug's got me woozy on the Taco Hell line. Between orders, I write lyrics about war and death. At the top of the page I write "Meat Grinder" and call it a song. I go to the bathroom and stare at the piss-spattered toilet, paper towels wadded behind chrome pipes. Maybe I'll never get the money, never get the amp, never get anywhere.

After I vomit and clean myself up, I go to the walk-in to cool my face and neck and imagine living off the stacked boxes of meat bags, shredded lettuce and cheese.

"Things getting too hot for you, baby?" Pam closes the door behind her until it clicks.

Pam is terrifying, her hair heavy-looking as chain mail, her skin impossibly pale in the freezer lights. She grinds against me, gropes the back of my leg and the small of my back.

Perplexed, she says, "Where is your butt?"

"I don't have one."

Just then, Marlon's seemingly disembodied head appears behind her. It floats away but he cracks the door for escape.

Pam says, "That's okay, honey," and licks her lips and plants them on mine.

This should feel epic. People go to war for love and sex, but mostly I feel a void. It stretches down a dark county road to a great house where my family was supposed to live together, a place I can never reach.

She jumps when Marlon screams into the walk-in, "PHONE CALL, PAMELA!"

"You're getting me hot, honey, even in the freezer." She takes off my hat, pats my head and puts it back.

After she leaves, I grab bags of lettuce and cheese for the line. I throw up again in the corner and this perfect steaming puddle loses its sheen in the cold.

Rick and Mom ask me to dinner. In the six months they've been dating they've never taken me anywhere. I hide my pentagram necklace from Spencer's Gifts under my t-shirt and tie my hair back. I grab Cliff's skull ring for luck.

We drive to Blake's Burger Veranda. I don't know what a veranda is and neither does Blake, who perches on a high stool with his arms crossed like a pudgy middle-aged lifeguard. All the tables have Heinz ketchup and plastic salt-and-pepper shakers, everything sticky. Greasy cheese squirts out of the buns and the fries are like ribbed fingers.

Rick eyes my skull ring when Mom's in the bathroom. "Where'd you get that, buddy?"

"The getting place."

He laughs like a cough. His eyes tell me he wants to say something else about the ring. He wants Mom to think he's so free and easy when that's horseshit.

She comes back to the table. "Sammy," she says, "we wanted to talk to you."

I press fries into my peppered ketchup smudge.

"Yeah, buddy! We got the best news!"

"Honey, how would you like Rick to be your stepdad?" Mom smiles at him like it's the best present they could give.

I consider the men Mom has brought home, the nose

grabbers, the ear-quarter magicians, the guys smashing cans on their foreheads. Grease monkeys using our garage to house their engine blocks. I love Mom, but why Rick? Why now? Doesn't matter what I think, it's a done deal. I stare Rick dead in the eyes. "How about you buy me that amp, stepdaddy?"

"What?" Rick laughs. He tries to whistle but can't find a tone. "You want something bad enough, boy, you gotta earn it. Or else you don't want it bad enough." He turns up his beer and knocks on the table like the case is closed. Mom squeezes his bicep.

"Can I have a beer?"

Mom squints at me.

"Well *shit!*" Rick says. "We're celebrating over here."

"Oh, Rick," she says.

"And we're headed to Mexico for a damn week, Sammy!"

"Great," I say.

He gets the waitress to bring me a Miller Lite, thinks it's my first. Clifftallica drinks it even though it tastes like crap. Rick slaps me on the back, he's so happy, and his fingers brush the pentagram chain.

Locusts scream from the trees like the sky is falling. He gets the jukebox going with "Rapper's Delight." On the deck Mom and Rick dance under floodlights.

I sip my beer and hate love even harder.

Loretta's working the front and we're slow. Stragglers and weirdos loiter in the dining area asking for pico and hot sauce. I'm perfecting "Meat Grinder" on the line when the paper gets jerked from under me. I wheel around on Loretta's full-lip grin. She goes to the long, skinny mic.

"Attention," she announces. "Sammy would like you to hear his song."

Marlon and Pam come over to listen. Customers look up.

Something nails me to the tile I'm standing on.

"Death and destruction
bodies crunchin
death is what we do
we do it well."

Marlon has to cover his face to keep from laughing. Something comes from my mouth that sounds like *ehrrrmmmmmm*.

"We'll cut your throat
we'll sink your boat
soon you'll feel the flames
the flames of hell."

I float above my dumb body. Marlon grins up at my spirit, flips it off.

"Loretta," Pam says, "if Sammy doesn't want you reading his poem, then stop."

"It's not a poem," I say.

Loretta smirks like this murder scene is cute. I grab my lyric sheet, so insane with embarrassed rage I've got half an erection. The rest of the shift, I feel wild and lost.

When I get home, there's a note:

Sammy,
We're off to Acapulco! TV dinners and frozen pizza in the freezer.
Love ya!
-Mom
PS: Don't whack it too much! -Rick

That weekend, we take the shrooms. Harold buys a garbage bag
of Colt 45 from Ziggler for forty bucks. We explode hot dogs in
the microwave and let the trash overflow and crouch over a Ouija
board to summon forth the dark lord. When Harold tries to drive
home, he revs the engine and throws it in reverse so hard the
transmission falls out in the cul-de-sac.

We roll around in the front yard laughing.

I wake up on the couch with my mouth open. Dawn breaks
gray over the trees and somebody is knocking. I open the door to a
silhouette I think is Cliff until I see the dad-shaped body. Then my
groggy mind says *Wayne* even though I hardly remember him. For a
moment I feel relief, like waking from a dream you're happy is only
a dream, like maybe I can make it somewhere no matter the doubt
I feel. No matter if I quit Taco Hell before I make enough money
for the amp. No matter how much life sucker punches you.

"I'm looking for Harold Gladney," the man says. He's got
square glasses, nothing like the picture of Wayne in the yellow Z28
with T-tops.

"Yes, sir."

I close the door in his face.

Harold is sprawled in my mother's bathroom in his tighties.
He cuddles a loaf of Wonder Bread. I toe his ass cheek until he
wakes up.

"Your old man is here."

"Shit," he says, sitting up. "What am I going to do?" He stares
at the loaf like it might tell him.

I toss him Rick's mangled toothbrush. "Brush your teeth,"
I say. "Be cool." He hardly uses any toothpaste and dribbles like
a goon.

Harold says goodbye. I watch from the window, hoping his father tears him a new one about the ruined transmission. On the front walk, he puts an arm around him and guides him to a new Oldsmobile, not like a cop, but like someone who cares where you are and what you do.

I'm so pissed, I go upstairs and turn up every knob on my tiny amp. I don't even want the big amp. Can't see what good it'll do.

News of Cobain's death drowns out everything. Kurt Loder and MTV News is a concentration camp of grief.

Marlon is dragging garbage to the dumpster when I arrive for my shift tripping on the last of the shrooms. We heft the bags into its leaky mouth. He stares at me, his face slack and blank. "That white boy rockstar killed hisself."

The streetlight over the lot buzzes like a microwave.

"Cobain," he says. "He killed hisself. And now all the white kids are killing theyselves." Marlon pulls out the longest cigarette I've ever seen and lights it. "White kids all over the country just blowing they heads off." He peers at me through his smoke, one eye opening larger than the other. "You ain't gonna kill yourself, are you?"

He left behind a baby girl and millions of crushed fans. Cobain blew so many things I want out the back of his head.

"Naw," I say. "Dude was lame."

Marlon laughs. We go inside.

Pam senses weakness and puts me at the back drive where I take money and hand out napkins and sauce packets. Boxes of fountain drink syrup are piled around me while customers smile through the window, murderous. Between orders, I feel eyes on my back.

"Mmm," Pam says. "Looking good tonight, Sammy. I'm gonna

need to see you in my office before you clock out." A smile spreads across her face like she might swallow my whole head.

"Yes, ma'am." Sweat blooms all over me as she backs away.

That's when the black Cadillac El Dorado rolls up, its hood so long I don't think I'll ever see the driver. Then there's cheap sunglasses, the denim jacket against the blood-red interior, reddish-brown hair to the tits.

Cliff pinches a joint into the ashtray and holds in the last hit. "They told me to pick you up."

I hang the headset on the rack.

The Cadillac's back seat aligns with my window. I climb through the drive-thru onto springy leather. I toss my hat in the bushes, pull out my hair tie, slide into the passenger seat.

Cliff turns up the radio. The opening of "Blackened" rises from the speakers, the first song on the album they put out after he died. Cliff's distorted wah-wah ghost-bass snarls out of the fade-in.

"This is what *Justice* was supposed to sound like," he says.

I peak. A wave of blue heat engulfs me.

Loretta gawks as we ease by at parade speed. I blow a metal kiss, fluttering it to her cheek.

Max Hipp

FUGITIVES

Pritchard used the biscuit to sop up the last of his egg-and-sausage plate. He drank coffee and slouched in his uniform at a two-seater by the kitchen while diners waddled down the narrow hall between the back and the main room. The Enid Valley paper seemed to shrink in size with each printing, and he skimmed a letter to the editor he had no interest in, a rant about the town's outdated liquor laws, because he liked the smell of newsprint. A man in a fishing shirt greeted Pritch as he passed the table and Pritch wondered if he'd ever seen the man before. Even if people didn't know him, they spoke to his badge and gun with a deference that always made him uncomfortable.

Something black floated under the cubes in his half-empty water glass. He rattled the ice, uncovering a fat fly with its legs folded, and pushed the glass to the far corner of the table. He didn't want to know what diseases flies carried. It was best to pretend it never happened, and he quickly firewalled it from his thoughts.

The bells on the aluminum doors jingled as he was refolding the paper. There, back from their honeymoon and waiting by the gumball machines to be seated, stood Doreen and Captain Will Campbell. She wore a green dress with no bra—it crushed Pritch to see her nipples when she didn't love him anymore. Pining for her was beyond reason, yet knowing this didn't unhook her towlines from his ribcage.

Will looked fit and rested. The bastard had run along Highway 8 until his beer belly melted down like a block of ice. He slicked his white hair to the side and shaved his beard to a neat goatee. He was in his mid-sixties but walked now with his shoulders back, his pants tighter, in a slimmer cut. That was Doreen's effect on him, when she hadn't so much as changed her lipstick. Pritch put it together once she stayed out all night and left him a note that read, "A lady's got to make her own way," and Will had come to the station the next morning humming. Pritch already put in his two weeks but had dragged his feet on finding police work elsewhere, thinking she might back out of marrying the old fart. Now that longshot was spent.

The waitresses never made him pay. He folded a ten-dollar bill and placed it under the fly water.

At the end of the dining room, they were sitting on the same side of the booth, backs to the bathrooms, his arm around her while she squinted over the menu, still too vain and stubborn to buy reading glasses. Will frowned when he saw Pritch coming past the register, then lifted his hand four inches off the table to wave.

Doreen never looked up.

Pritch nodded and went out the jangling door.

Around two, he turned north from the depot onto Main Street. He passed the Kitty Cat Inn where a white boy in a black hoodie darted across the parking lot and leaned against the motel's yellow stucco. His cargo short pockets bulged with—what? Pill bottles? Wads of cash? Recent break-ins had brought the Belden sisters down to the police station complaining about missing heirloom rings, so Pritch wheeled the patrol car into the lot and flashed the siren in a quick *blu-ruuuuuuuuuu!* It caused the boy to stiffen as if electrocuted and slide down the wall.

He pulled up slow, bumping tires against a parking stop, and spat like a snake into the lip of a twenty-ounce plastic bottle, thankful the boy didn't run off in the muddy lot between the gas station and the high school. He gripped the roof of the car to hoist his two hundred twenty pounds, plus forty more of vest, belt, and gun, out of the seat, every ounce attacking his popping knees. Trying to appear larger, he squared his shoulders and approached the boy, who was only seven or eight but tall for his age.

"What's going on, pal?"

The boy's eyes were clear but roving. He smelled like a grubby nickel.

When he didn't respond, Pritch pulled him gently by the hood until he was standing. He mashed the pockets and, hearing paper crinkle, made him empty them. Wadded pages fell on the pavement. Pritch stomped a few before they blew away. Bible pages.

"You tore up a Bible?" Pritch had had one with a blue cover and his name printed inside. He remembered the smell of the ink, how each leaf felt almost transparent.

"Mama tore it from the nightstand." The boy's voice almost a bleat. "Told me to read stories if I got scared."

"She stuffed Bible pages in your pocket and left?"

The boy nodded.

His own mother had never, to his knowledge, defaced a Bible, though she tried to wreck him other ways. Pritch raised his eyebrows and half-smiled to look friendlier.

"You got a name?"

"Bev."

"That your real name?"

"Yessir."

Pritch told him to stuff the pages back in his pocket and not let any blow away or he'd be busted for littering. Bev complied without complaint, a good boy, really, who deserved better than this. Pritch's mother had abandoned him sometimes for days. In dark moments, he still remembered her backing the car out of the driveway at midnight, late to meet god-knows-who, the claustrophobia of a childhood spent petrified with worry.

"Where do you live?"

Bev pointed at the wall.

Pritch plopped a half-dollar of tobacco spit on the walkway. He'd wanted to get off early and shoot the Browning Buck Mark he'd bought at the Tupelo Gun Show. That would have to wait.

"We're going to sort you out," Pritch said. He glanced at the lazy traffic on Main Street in time to see Doreen's rusting Subaru Outback drive by.

Though it stood six hours north of the nearest shore, the Kitty Cat Inn was painted beach colors. Yellow stucco with turquoise room doors. A cat head drawn in red on each door, one eye as the peephole. Pritchard knocked. The curtains didn't sway. Folks stayed at the Kitty Cat for extended periods, like Pritch had when Doreen kicked him out for getting drunk and throwing her car keys on the roof. That had been in their early days together, the ones he missed the most. He couldn't believe it was only two years ago.

He shifted his weight from one foot to the other, still holding the boy by the hood. Bev slouched in his clean-enough second-hand clothes.

"How long you been here?"

Bev stuck out his lip and shrugged. The misfirings behind his eyes and his parted lips gave him the appearance of constant astonishment. His demeanor was friendly enough that his silence didn't bother Pritch. He led him to the car. The boy watched him spit brown into the plastic bottle and then they stepped over dead shrubs and through the pneumatic doors of the lobby, where a twenty-year-old girl leaned against the counter.

"Could you tell me if anyone's in room 166?"

She clacked on the keyboard for a while, like she wasn't checking what Pritch asked for at all. Then she said, "Checked out this morning. Already clean."

"What's the name?"

The girl squinted. "Tonya Harding."

"The knee whacker?"

"I watched a documentary about that," she said. "What a coincidence, right?"

Bev stood at the rack of yellowed dogeared postcards. He sniffed one and put it back.

"Unbelievable," Pritch said.

Will leaned against Pritch's door facing. He gestured to Bev, who was drawing on a manila folder with markers.

"What's this about?"

Prichard put the phone back in the cradle. "His mother left him at the Kitty Cat. I'm trying to track her down."

"If it's a missing person, we need to call it in as one."

Pritch uncrossed his leg under the metal desk, kicking the underside. His two weeks couldn't pass quickly enough. He closed his eyes and said, "We're going to have to gather some information first. That okay with you?"

Will stepped one linoleum square into the office. But only one.

"You want something else?" Pritch asked. He hoped the old man wanted to fight. A fight would simplify things. Might even help matters.

"You've got barbecue sauce on the corner of your mouth."

Pritch snatched a brown paper towel from a stack on his desk. He stared at Will as he scratched it against the whiskers around his lips. The residue was tobacco colored. Bev had let him walk around with tobacco spit on his face without saying anything. That hurt a little.

"You might need protective services on this. They're set up to take care of boys."

The back of Pritch's neck went slick with grime as he fought the urge to call him a Viagra-popping sapsucker. "I suspect I'll handle it."

Will ran his hand over his goatee as if to wring it. He said, "I suspect you will." Then he turned sideways, studying the floor on either side of his shoes.

"Hey," Pritch said, "the kid has a name."

Will stuck his head back in the room. "What's your name, son?"

"Bev."

"Isn't that a girl's name?"

Bev dropped the purple marker on the floor and picked up a yellow. He waited until Will shook his head and left before he said, "Nope."

Pritch whistled like a bomb drop.

Bev whistled it back and squiggled the marker.

While Bev went into McDonald's to pee, Pritch scrolled an app and saved a few beach pictures, a compulsion started while searching for places to visit with Doreen. Clearwater Beach, Panama City, Playa de Carmen, Cozumel. The names themselves felt like vacations in his mouth. The algorithms suggested new beaches to click on. He touched the pictures, rolled the wheel of light.

He always saw his future with Doreen like a drone over a yard: children on a swing set, her face beaming as she pushed. He wished to make her as happy as she was in his mind. With the Captain, her face wore contentment, close to beaming. Pritch had begged her to come back, then resigned himself that sometimes women left loyal men who loved them. It stung and would go on stinging. Other women abandoned children at motels and vanished into drugs, The Beaver Trap, or the Yalobusha River. He wanted to be wrong about what had happened to Bev's mother.

Bev popped the door and climbed in. He jerked the seatbelt and fastened it as fast as he could.

"Think you might want to be a policeman when you grow up?"

Bev nodded. He picked up the spit bottle and swirled the juice around the bottom. "How's spit get this color?"

Pritch snatched it. "You got to grow up before you can spit like this." He spat into it to demonstrate.

A pregnant woman angled herself into the car next to them. She fell panting into her seat, clutching a food bag.

"Looks gross," Bev said.

Housing projects stood outside of town where Bev said he might've lived, he wasn't sure. He fiddled with the console while Pritch drove, switched the radio off and on, poked at the computer stuck to the dash. They patrolled an older neighborhood gone bad sometime in the '80s during a similar but different drug epidemic. He told Bev to point out anything familiar. The rusted swing sets were familiar. A lightning-split tree. The basketball goal made from a bucket rim screwed to a table top bolted to a telephone pole. They stopped and shot a flat basketball at the hoop a few times before Bev lost interest and knelt to make a roly-poly curl. Bev didn't seem to understand where he'd come from, like he dropped from the sky over Kitty Cat Inn. If Jesus could rise after three days, if mankind could assemble atomic weapons and alien ships could fly out of the Gulf of Mexico, then a strange boy could fall from the sky unharmed.

Pritch turned the stereo to a classic rock station playing Rod Stewart. He hated Rod Stewart, but his mother would sing "Maggie May" when he was sick with stomachaches. She'd turn up the stereo and sing true, her raspy angel voice blowing their troubles out the window. For a song, at least.

He drove past a scatter of trailers, near replicas of places he'd lived with his mother. He could roll through and find crimes everyone at the station had grown tired of stopping. People would beat and rob and use each other whether police intervened or not, Pritch suspected. Why they couldn't do like he'd done and lift themselves up, take their fragments elsewhere to make themselves whole, he had no idea.

They pulled down a cul-de-sac and Bev bolted upright. Under a slanted mimosa, a half-trailer loomed, scorched on one end, windows stuffed with swollen cardboard. Pritch pulled over.

"Ever been here?"

Bev kept his eyes fixed on the dash and slouched. "No, sir." The car suddenly reeked of dirty coins.

"You wouldn't lie to me, would you?"

Bev shook his head. Sweat had beaded in his toothbrush-bristle hair.

Pritch never wanted to go home after school to the curtain-less place where his mother lit cigarettes and forgot them. The couch caught fire while she was passed out once. He filled a pot and doused it and she slapped him for getting everything wet. Then they took that place, and even her, away.

"We'll keep patrolling," Pritch said.

Out on Highway 8, he saw Will's fat mailbox. This was the vacuum mouth of failure, the last place he needed to go. He decided to turn in, and Bev glanced at him as if he knew something of failure too.

The driveway wound through trees and opened onto century-old pastureland where a large cabin with gray chinking between ancient pine logs stood like a relic from another world. A lake glimmered beyond it and two great herons hunted in the tall grass. Even if she wasn't home, they could watch turtles slide off the logs.

Doreen stepped onto the long porch in pink tennis shoes and workout clothes that showed her midriff. Pritch's eyes watered. He wanted to draw a bath to soak her, drink the water and lick her clean like a cat. Then he remembered the boy. Somehow Bev inspired him not to debase himself. In the moment between turning the engine off and getting out, he figured this was the effect fatherhood might've had on him, a centering in the world.

They got out and closed their doors at the same time.

"Am I under arrest, officers?"

"Yes," Bev announced.

A yellow lab ran from under plywood propped against the cabin, straight to Bev. He knelt and it licked his face. It capered into the yard, wanting to be chased.

"Get him," Doreen said.

Pritch told him to stay close. Boy and dog ran toward the lake, already pals.

"Will wouldn't like this one bit." She rolled her eyes.

He followed her into the kitchen. She placed two glasses on the table and poured from a pitcher of lemonade. Bits of pulp swirled in the cloudy water like sea monkeys.

"What's with the kid?"

"Can't find his mother."

"What's he doing at my house?

Pritch pinched his earlobe. He could fill a book with what he didn't know and didn't know how to write a book either. He sat at the table with his great love who no longer wanted him.

"I'd do anything to get you back."

"That's why you came by?" She laughed. "Pritch, we've been through this every which way."

"Tell me you don't miss me then." Their history bucked under his stomach. He prepared to recount minute details of their lovemaking if needed. The way panties sliding down her stubbled thighs, for instance, sounded like sugar pouring into hot coffee.

She reached for the counter and came back with her phone. She scrolled through something and set it facedown. "I can't drag every old thing into the light today. I know you do it all the time, but it wears me out."

So calmly, she said the things that shook him.

"Our past together doesn't mean anything to you?"

She tapped her seafoam green nails on the table for a moment. "You hang onto the past like it's all you've got." She squinted at the bright window. "The past, to me, is just what I let go of."

The front door slammed open. Bev and the yellow dog barreled in.

Doreen poured water for the dog and a glass of lemonade for Bev. The dog lapped from the bowl and sloshed all over the kitchen.

"What do you think, cutie?" Doreen asked. "You care anything about the past?"

An icy feeling crept up Pritch's shoulders and pricked his ears.

"No, ma'am," said Bev.

Pritch stopped at the turnaround at the county dump. A ripped, cushionless couch leaned on the hillside. Scattered beer cans and cardboard boxes hung in the weeds. A roaring log truck rocked the car as Bev's pee stream shot ahead ten feet.

                                    Max Hipp

He tried to conjure a better mood by picturing Doreen on a beach somewhere, white sand and Windex-blue water. It was no use. Maybe a small town far away needed an experienced deputy, but he'd grown used to the discomfort of Doreen and Will, and the idea of change pulsed like a hot balloon under his heart.

The radio hissed. "That boy's a runaway from Panola County," the new dispatcher said. "Looks like he made everything up."

Bev did a shimmy somebody had taught him and zipped up. Pritch remembered the fly in the ice and a faint tension registered in his jaw, like he was listening to distant, unpleasant music. He grabbed the handset, said, "Copy that."

He stared at the woods, where he could see Bev's future clear as his own past: foster homes, a few state-run. The powdered eggs and rubbery potatoes, the watery half-pints of milk. A cot for a bed, or a metal frame and springs with the thinnest stained mattress. He'd stumble into adulthood strange and misshapen. Enemies in every corner.

Bev opened the door.

"Still want to be a policeman?" Pritch asked.

He nodded.

"Then go get those cans." He reached under his seat and pulled out the Browning Buck Mark. "We're going to learn to shoot."

Bev side-eyed the polished wood and blue barrel of the gun and left the door ajar. Pritch thought maybe the gun scared him until he plucked the first crushed can from the weeds.

The radio crackled with Will's voice. "Pritch, bring the boy back. They've got security footage of him shoplifting at Fred's."

Crumpled Bible pages were mashed into the crack of the seat like a packrat had nested. Pritch opened a wad.

He has also set eternity in the human heart—

He smoothed out another: *I have told you these things, so that in me you may have peace. In this world you will have trouble. But take heart! I have overcome the world.*

He balled up the pages and tossed them on the floorboard.

On the hill, Bev gathered dented cans in his shirt like Easter eggs. Pritch wanted to show him how to sight the white bead on the target. The satisfying *thunk* of bullets entering aluminum.

He tucked the .22 under his belt and climbed out of the cruiser, feeling everything in his knees.

They rode into town at dusk, past Super Hair World and Piggly Wiggly. Bev hardly missed a shot once he understood the mechanics of the Buck Mark's sight. His cheeks were pink from smiling so much. Pritch considered other things he could teach him. Accident reports were easy to fill out, and anybody could check the boxes for speeding tickets.

As he approached the station, Brenda from child services was out front talking to Will.

Pritch said, "Next thing a lawman has to learn is how to wash his vehicle."

"Yessir," Bev said.

The Captain stood before the double doors. He watched them with his arms wide like he was ready to draw his sidearm.

Pritch locked eyes with him as he pressed the accelerator and passed the station, headed for car wash stalls at the edge of town.

MAD LOVE

Boyd couldn't stand another sub sandwich from Lou's, not even with the employee discount. At the new fusion taco place across town, in the middle of rundown houses with rents going up, he parked across the street, under a black-and-white sign that read Hector's Limousines & Formalwear. He backed his beater Accord into the shade and went to lunch.

Thirty minutes later his car was gone.

He could hear Lilla, his wife, clucking her tongue. Now he had to pick up Alex from the in-laws with no car, her parents waiting in the driveway next to the gleaming Mercedes they paid someone to detail. And if he called Lou to tell him he'd be late getting back, Lou would stamp out his Swisher and rip off his greasy Devil Rays hat, bow his head in prayer for better employees.

Boyd read the HECTOR'S ONLY signs screwed to the posts in front of the spaces and glared at the point of the A-frame roof. He went to counseling he couldn't have afforded without health insurance through his adjunct job teaching the future hedge fund managers of Tampa Bay how to communicate. This grad student in Crocs taught him to count breaths, in through the nose, out the mouth, and it felt like a superpower. After a few seconds, it calmed him.

He opened the doors to racks of gowns and tuxedoed mannequins in spotlights along the wall. A bald man in a tie and short-sleeve button-down sat at a high desk. He had thick eyelids, a spritz of freckles. Neck fat bulged over his collar, but rather than froglike, he looked regal somehow. Boyd had this urge to punch him in the ribs.

"I parked in your lot and got towed."

The man's smile melted. He squinted and motioned toward the taco place. "They didn't build enough spaces and I've got to run a business. What am I supposed to do?"

A woman in a white blouse was sitting behind the low partition. Honey-colored eyes, olive complexion. Her hair seemed windblown yet sculpted in place. "It was one car, Hector. One car."

"One car?" Hector's voice rose in pitch. "One car is just the start."

"I didn't notice," the woman said to Boyd. "But my husband notices everything." She made a face like she might spit. "He's a busybody."

"B & B Towing," Hector the busybody said to Boyd.

Outside, phone to his ear, he stared at the cracked concrete where he'd parked, the fence and the tall grass beyond it, the underbrush backed up to swamps. If he could trudge into the muck and lie in it, it might feel cool and comforting on his skin. He rented an apartment close to Lou's, with a balcony overlooking a gas station where a dude leaned against a light pole every night, selling something, while Lilla and Alex lived in the house without him. He and Lilla loved each other but weren't *in love* and discussed this often on the phone.

B & B Towing said the driver was probably at lunch with his car hooked to the winch, and he wouldn't be able to get it until later. It would cost two hundred fifty dollars. Through the glass, the woman made wide sweeping gestures at Hector. He went back in and asked the number for a taxi just to look at her again.

"Wait a minute," she said. She came from behind the partition, tall and thick-hipped. "I'm headed out anyway. I can drive you."

Hector said, "Let the grown man solve his problems."

She gave him a disgusted look. She was maybe six or eight years older than Boyd, into her late forties with no visible lines in her face. Or maybe she covered them well.

"Actually," Boyd said, "I could use the ride."

She drove them in a vintage limo. Boyd sat up front, the air freshener like pink bubblegum, the leather seats dull but detailed and cared for. She pulled the long car slowly off the lot.

"Check your vent." She adjusted the AC controls and pointed toward his door. "It gets closed sometimes. Me, I'm always hot. I'm Agatha, by the way."

The vent whipped hot air in his face and blew back her department store perfume. He couldn't remember the last time he'd ridden anywhere with a woman other than Lilla, and it had been so long since they'd touched in any meaningful way. He'd pushed his feelings about that down the well and was pulling them out again, bucket by bucket, for the counselor, who kept saying to turn toward pain. Turn toward it instead of away.

"Hector gets stupid ideas about right and wrong." She stopped at the intersection. "So pigheaded." A beat later the east-west traffic started. "The last thing entering his mind is giving somebody a break."

"It's okay." It wasn't okay, but bitching wouldn't help.

"Well, you're taking this better than most." Her high cheekbones shined in the glare off the bumpers and windshields. "Are you some kind of saint?"

"My ex would say no."

"But you've got a coolness, like not much gets to you. A cool customer. Cool as a cucumber."

"Too cool for school."

A low, sugary laugh rose from her chest.

They passed a used car dealership and signs for the Mexican bakery. He held the Spanish words for *ice cream* and *store* in his mouth, flicking his tongue tip against his teeth. A few short blocks and Agatha's scent would go away with the AC. Between the car getting towed and the situation with Lilla, he felt like a stew set to boil, overflowing any moment. The idea he was cool had never crossed his mind.

She glided into the turn lane, studied the side mirrors. The thought of finishing his double shift in the humid restaurant sank him in the leather. Another night alone followed by another double. Alex would get bored with the toys at his apartment. He'd charge the towing fee and pay the minimum on the credit card for another month, then go to the college to teach people, who'd make more money than he'd ever see, to write a business email. He'd probably need a third job to keep the apartment with the gas station view and the dope man.

She pulled in front of Lou's. "Here you go, stranger." She slapped his knee and two seconds of heat spread up his thigh, left a light sheen of sweat on his back. "You didn't tell me your name."

"Boyd Blatt."

She cocked her head and squinted, repeated his full name twice. He popped open the door.

"Wait a minute," she said. "It's going to cost you." She glanced at the sign. Somebody had smashed the u in *sub* with a rock. "Let me reimburse you."

Boyd told her he'd done the wrong thing and planned to pay

for it. He had two minutes to clock in. He got out and ducked his head in to get another look at her broad shoulders and bright eyes. A woman like that could make you feel like somebody else in your skin.

"I want to take you out sometime," he said, not believing he'd said it.

Her laugh went high then low, melodious. She beat the steering wheel. It wasn't funny enough to beat the steering wheel.

"The last thing I need is another man complicating my life." Then she pointed at him with her long nails. "What you need is a friend. I'll be your friend, Boyd Blatt."

"Sure." He rolled his eyes. "Okay."

"You don't believe?" She asked his number. He figured she was pretending to put it in her phone. "Gonna call you."

"You don't have to. You can lose my number and no hard feelings."

"Not a chance."

He slammed the door harder than he meant to. She waved.

For a week afterward, he worked at Lou's, taught classes, and daydreamed about taking Agatha's limo down to Sarasota or Fort Myers Beach. He wanted the ocean brine on her skin and the sun on her scalp. He wanted her to provide what was missing, things the counselor said could only come from within him. He'd imagine unbuckling her belt, her thighs against his lips. The counselor never explained how those missing things might come from within him. He was ready to *turn toward* something like that.

Lou took a break and left him to work the front and back at once. Most of the customers were takeout, except for Mr. Ng, who lumped his taxi hat on the Formica table. He ordered a Rancho Deluxe and sat for hours with reading glasses on the end of his nose, doing sudoku. No one ever joined him. Boyd walked into the cooler full of processed meat and awful cheeses Lou wouldn't throw away and considered how much time Mr. Ng spent alone, wondering if he rolled cigarettes on his balcony at night too. He remembered a trip to the beach when Alex was a baby, when he and Lilla were like other couples. Alex was five now. He wouldn't grow up with any scenes of his mom and dad holding hands in line for snow cones.

On Sundays they ate dinner together. They sat at the table, watched TV until one of them tucked Alex in. Then Boyd went to his apartment to roll one cigarette in the dark and watch the man smoke under the gas station light, the man with full pockets and infinite patience. He leaned against the pole with self-possession, detached and satisfied, like he was born to lean and wait. Boyd wondered what magic he sold.

He made a Torpedo Supremo for a takeout order, cut the wheat roll, slapped on Mexican mayonnaise, laid on turkey and Swiss and avocado with a squeeze of lime. It was slippery with the gloves. He almost dropped the sandwich but wrapped it, stapled the receipt to the bag, and set it next to Lou's Dr. Zaius action figure by the register.

Lou walked in and said, "A card came for you."

"From who?"

He slammed the broiler closed. "How the hell should I know?" He dragged the garbage can out back.

Boyd found it in the bill basket by the dusty coffeemaker, addressed to Boyd Blatt at Lou's Sub Shop from Hector's Limousines & Formalwear. Enclosed was Agatha Gutierrez's sales manager card and a gift certificate for a one-hour full-body massage at Mad Love. Instead of signing the back, she sketched a smiley face with sunglasses and wrote FOR A COOL CUSTOMER.

                                    Max Hipp

Mad Love glowed inside a neon heart fastened in a window between a laundromat and a title loans place. Boyd followed a short, stocky woman named Cindy into the back.

They came to a room with blackout curtains over the windows and an intense lavender scent. She stood next to a blanketed table with a donut-shaped cushion protruding from the end.

"Anything specific today?"

His face flushed. "I've never had a massage."

She stood on her toes and lowered herself back down. "Then we'll just do a full body and address problem areas on the fly." She turned around at the door. "So now I'll go and you'll disrobe and lie face down with your nose and mouth through that." She waved to the donut. "You can leave your underwear on or off. Doesn't matter to me as long as you're comfortable."

When she closed the door, windchime music started playing from ceiling speakers. Other than the table, there was only a large dresser with lots of cabinets. He stuffed his socks inside his shoes and placed them on the floor in the corner, draped his pants over them. He put his wallet, phone, keys, and pocketknife on the pants, and folded his t-shirt on top.

Cindy knocked and came in. She tucked the covers into the waistband of his boxers, then squirted oil from a bottle and rubbed her wet hands together. She pushed her fingers into his lower back muscles with all her weight. His nose, eyes, and mouth were through the donut hole, its hard metal frame pressing against his cheeks and forehead.

"So you're friends with Agatha?"

He had to get his face out of the cushion to answer yes.

"She comes in every week for a full body. She's a great human, if you ask me."

He grunted as Cindy's thumbs dug in. Agatha's body had pressed against this table, and Cindy had pressed her in the same places. He lay silent as images gently swept through his mind. Agatha driving them over the Sunshine Skyway. Agatha in a lowcut nightie. He was almost dreaming. As Cindy pressed deeply into his neck and shoulders, it was like drifting along on her river of touch.

One of her hands went for oil again while the other stayed in place. His mind flashed with his old car, rusted blue and silver, his dog, General, he'd had twenty years back. The parking lot dude walked up to beaters with their windows rolled down. Faces of disgraced politicians blinked in and out. TV snow. Everything appeared bright and vivid and then blurred like Polaroids sinking into a swimming pool. It was hard to focus on anything before it was gone. She ran her arm under his shoulder and pressed, her belly brushing his palm. One moment she was pushing the limits of pain in each muscle, and in the next, gently turning his body or carefully squeezing his fingers.

A cabinet opened. She tucked the blanket under his thighs and reached for the oil again, kept one hand resting on his heel. She worked each leg, kneading electric lines up his hamstrings, to the tops of his feet. He turned over and she swung his arm across his chest, plucked knots in his neck, her ragged breath in his ear. Tears raced from both his eyes.

When time was up, she whispered, "Take your time, honey," and left.

He sat up feeling stoned. Framed pictures of Cindy with her kids stood on the dresser. They rode bikes in a park. They mugged in the sun on the edge of a canyon.

His clothes were piled in the corner like he'd melted there.

Before Sunday dinner that weekend, he taught Alex to tie his shoes.

Now he was sitting in front of the TV, eyes on the screen, untying and retying them without looking, a fast learner. Sometimes Boyd felt Alex didn't need him at all, but he'd learned thoughts like those came from self-hate.

The air thickened with fried chicken and simmered butterbeans. Lilla tonged the chicken onto paper towels to blot the grease.

"You look good," she said. She'd covered the gray streaks by going blonder. "Rested."

When he told her about the massage at Mad Love, she put down the tongs. "How did that happen?" She stirred the beans. "I mean, I never knew you were interested in massages."

"I didn't know until I went."

Her face seemed pensive in the yellow light beneath the microwave. "I can't imagine you booking an appointment."

"My friend Agatha gave me a gift certificate."

"Agatha?" Her nose crinkled so fast someone else would've missed it. "Where'd you meet Agatha?"

He explained the new taco shop on the gentrified side of town, leaving out the tow truck, the tense ride with Lou to B & B Towing, and the money it cost. He told her about Agatha's limo and formalwear business, how she thought he was funny.

"You *are* funny, Boyd," Lilla said. She banged the spoon against the pot. "I guess you just never know."

Alex went upstairs after dinner. They discussed who would pay the car note. His was paid for but hers was only a few years old, and they alternated payments each month. He explained he was short. He didn't tell her it was because of the tow charge.

"Boyd," she said. "I don't know what to do with you sometimes."

This is the point when, if she found him lacking in some way, he used to lose his mind. "I can pick it up next month," he said. It was her car but she was still his wife, and in his head, this was what a husband taking care of a wife looked like. Paying for things.

"I know you're trying your best." She reached across the table, her eyes watery, and grabbed his hand. "You're my greatest love, Boyd Blatt." She squeezed his fingers.

They still said these things to each other. She wanted to hear *You're my greatest love too*. Or: *I love and miss you too*. But it wasn't clear what *greatest love* meant when love didn't want to live with you anymore.

He stared at their hands, how the fingers interwove. "Thanks for saying so." He pictured himself as an astronaut, floating off into space. Lilla's signals came through the static. But his didn't reach her at all. "It means a lot."

The light illuminated the rear of the gas station—back door, mop bucket on wheels, wet rubber mats, stacks of plastic soda crates. The man stood against the pole with his back to the complex like the residents were the least of his worries, but they could've called the cops. They were capable of anything.

Boyd sat in his camping chair on the balcony, feet propped on the iron rail. He rolled cigarettes by hand, though he never smoked the whole pouch of American Spirit before it went stale. Lilla didn't know about the smoking. He wanted to create a list of behaviors she didn't know about.

The dope man lit a cigarette and tilted his head back, exhaling at stars neither of them could see beyond the city glow. Agatha was probably in her house at that moment, counting the day's receipts from tuxes and limos, with Hector. The peace of long-married couples after work, the comfort of routine and easy touch. He imagined Lilla with the man who could make her happy, pictured his fresh haircut and tanning-bed face.

A car swung into the parking lot, turned off the headlights

                                                    Max Hipp

before they could shine on the man. He flicked his cigarette at the weeds and rubbed his neck. The driver's arm came out the window and they greeted each other like old friends. Twenty seconds later the car backed up and drove toward the dead mall. The man lit up again. He'd be fine, something else would come along.

It didn't matter anymore what he was selling. Boyd kept his cash tips in an old recipe box in the kitchen. He tucked forty dollars in his palm, a week's worth, walked downstairs and crossed the lot. The man turned around when he heard Boyd's shoes scuffing, but he didn't seem surprised.

DISCIPLES OF SUEDE

I lived with my mom and stepdad near the reservoir in a neighborhood called Waterwood where each house had the same worn-out, rotten-looking, gray-shingle exterior. When Suede first moved to Waterwood, the kids in junior high couldn't believe his weird name and called him Sweetie. That stuck until everyone got more creative, called him Blue Suede Shoes, Can't Get Laid Suede. Other than the name, he was forgettable.

Then, the summer before high school blessed him. He'd always had a large head, but he arrived in ninth-grade homeroom six-six and lean. Once he figured out he was bigger and stronger, he kicked Buck Simpson's ass for bullying him and got suspended. He returned to school, a new pecking order established overnight. Buck, until that point one of the populars, began to huddle and scowl with the skateboarders on the fringes of the soccer field.

Suede and I bonded when I found his missing cat, Belch. I'd recognized the tabby stripes from a hundred paces.

He opened his front door and eyed me like it was a trap.

"Your cat's on the road," I said, with proper solemnity.

We stepped through knee-high weeds to jump the ditch. Belch's orange collar had melted in the heat and stretched on the asphalt like chewing gum. We observed a moment of silence on the road shoulder as cars slowed to gawk.

He turned, eyes quivering like he might hit me. He shook my hand.

"I'm going to get a shovel," he said.

High school became the Suede show. On the junior-varsity basketball team, he could've played forward, center, or point-guard—didn't matter. Suede trounced the competition, assisting, faking, passing, alleyooping from hand to gargantuan hand for the slam. The rest of us were pivoting plywood boards to bounce the ball off before he scored, installed to provide the illusion of teamwork. We lined up afterward and chanted in the losers' faces, "Good game, good game, good game," but they were never good games.

In the beginning, he loved the adoration. He stayed an extra hour in grubby gymnasiums afterward just to jaw with old farts who waited to snap pictures with him. He got his face in the local paper with the headline: "New Star on the Horizon." As a forward on the soccer team, he jumped a foot higher than the other players and headed the ball into the netting. Each game was Suede's show and visiting teams were reluctant witnesses to his greatness.

Winning always bent him philosophical. On the bus ride back from away games, he'd sit on the half-seat with a sweaty cheerleader on his lap and proclaim, "The world is open. You've got to take what's yours while you can. None of us are here for long at all." He'd put a cigar in his mouth, fifteen years old. Nobody stopped him because he was bigger than the law.

I'd read my Homer and Ayn Rand. I wanted to be a warrior poet, a rich one.

We, myself and Suede's teammates, always believed we were better than everyone else, and his dominance eliminated any doubt.

At Suede's house, rows of curio cabinets displayed crystal and the grandfather clock chimed on the hours and half-pasts. Couch cushions bulged with stuffing. His father worked for a massive accounting firm in Jackson and his mother, Cindy Pickens, was a housewife who sewed buttons, wore an apron, cleaned his room, polished the silver. The off-white walls were free of scuffs even around the baseboards. We needed only mention a want in passing and it would appear on a TV tray wielded by Cindy, Queen of Waterwood, like she crouched around the corner, listening for her cue. She wore makeup and was shapely in the hips under the apron. I often pictured her riding a horse and wearing a wolf-pelt bikini.

My own house—my own life—was empty and pedestrian. My mother worked as a receptionist at a doctor's office and wore housecoats and slippers whenever home. My stepfather was a salesman for General Mills who would sit around in his underwear, polishing his Browning rifles. They'd invite me to watch HBO with them dressed like that. I'd shake my head and retreat to my room, ashamed. Even as I hid, I wore my best polo shirt, thinking of the future, always the future, because the present depressed the hell out of me.

At Suede's house, waiting for him to appear, I'd make small talk with Cindy. She named him after her favorite fabric to touch, just loved the sound of it. Once I asked her what she was doing that Saturday afternoon. Her eyes lit with tiny fires.

"Well," she said, "I've got Suede's lunch at one o'clock, baseball practice at three, and dinner at six. Then a glass of wine and off to bed."

She went on about Suede's future sports engagements. As I listened, I ogled her, tried to suck her through my pupils. Suede was truly master of his house. I took mental note of this for my future kingdom.

My father was stationed in Hawaii. He sent beach postcards I tacked on the bulletin board over the aquarium where I sometimes found dry twisted fish bodies stuck to the carpet and covered with ants. He wrote on the cards in thick black ink: HANG LOOSE! SURF'S UP!

In the garage my mother and stepfather constructed the biggest model train set of all time. They wore engineer hats and blew tiny whistles. New boxes of train track, railroad crossing signs, plastic mountains and trees kept appearing on our doorstep. My stepfather wanted real smoke to come out of the locomotives, so the garage and kitchen always smelled like burnt vegetable oil.

I'd sit in the loft over the living room, make paper airplanes and toss them into the ceiling fan. On good days I could get one stuck on each blade. No matter how much paper I wasted or how many planes wound up behind the sofa and entertainment center, my mother never mentioned it. By bedtime, she'd have the living room spic and span again, like none of us existed.

A year went by with Suede carrying our teams. Then, out of the blue, Becky Myrtletree became Suede's eternal love. To him, she was a queen, a between-class, hall-walking dream. He worshipped her cheekbones and fanny curve. To me, she wasn't much. Why settle for a Dixie Cup when you could have The Grail? But by the third movie date, they'd named their children: Penelope, Preston, Porgy, and Petunia.

In a brief phone call, he told me he'd met Becky's parents. Of course, they were smitten by the idea of an all-star son-in-law. But even in those halcyon days there was foreboding.

As tenth grade wore on, I began to see less of Suede, which felt cruel and mean. But nothing would be ordinary again. The unexpected seemed the price of admission.

"You know," he said one night on the phone, "I told Cindy not to sign me up for any more extracurriculars so I could go out with Becky. You'd have thought I'd slapped her. She sat on the kitchen floor a good hour."

"What was she wearing?" I couldn't help myself. My hormones were half-banshee and wailing.

"Sometimes," he said, "you're a total psycho."

A couple days later, we were sitting on the bleachers in P.E. and practicing our hook shots with wadded up notebook paper on the garbage can.

He said, "I told Cindy I was finished with basketball. She cried and begged me not to quit soccer, so I kept that one."

Soccer was the lesser sport, but I didn't say so. Suede was lopping off pieces of himself. The lack of coaching could only lead to aimlessness. What good was all that power without discipline? I imagined him twiddling his thumbs, staring out windows into darkness. Immortality within reach, yet he turned away, like if Icarus nosedived on purpose before he could even melt.

"What are you going to do with yourself?"

He hummed for a minute and said, "Whatever hurts my folks the most."

I began cutting women out of magazines. The aprons, the lips, the violin shapes. I extracted images from my mother's *Cosmopolitans* and *People Magazine*s. With an X-Acto knife, paste, and poster board I assembled a shrine to Cindy Pickens. My mother barged in my room while I was culling from her magazines one day. I scrambled to hide the scraps, realized it was futile, and sat frozen.

I'd cut from some of my stepdad's forgotten *Playboys* and felt lucky I'd tucked those between the pages of *The Fountainhead* and *Children of Dune.*

"Oh." She picked up some of the cutouts. "Very nice."

We never laid hands on each other in our family, but she touched my hair, frightening me.

"Do what you love, sweetheart," she said. "Do what you love."

She left and went out to the garage, electric trains whining forlornly along the tracks, and closed the door.

The finished collage looked nothing like Cindy, but I worked until something about it stood my arm hairs on end. Then I put The Doors' *L.A. Woman* on repeat and sat for hours, stared at the poster-board shrine, dreamed of the future. Once I earned my fortune I could make her mine.

One night when Suede was out with Becky, I went to see Cindy. She answered the door in her apron, lipstick freshly applied and glistening. I almost jumped her in the foyer, with Suede's dad watching TV in the living room, but pulled myself together.

"I'm worried about him," I said.

Her lashes moistened with tears. She grabbed my hand—the touch burned into the crotch of my heart—and led me to the den.

"He won't be my Suede anymore!"

"It's like he's lost!" I said.

"He's wasting his life on…on…that *bitch*!"

The venom in her voice stopped my blood. Her face twisted around the word, and for a moment I didn't recognize her. She composed herself, apologized for swearing, and went on.

"Fighting with me. Locking his bedroom door. Not letting me wash his clothes anymore. He told me he doesn't want to go to college. He just wants to roam the country, work whatever job

                                                    Max Hipp

there is." She brought a handkerchief out of her apron pocket and cried into it. "That's not our plan!"

"There, there," I said, patting her luscious knee. I had no idea what *there, there* meant but actors comforting actresses sure did. She leaned against me and cried. I tried to cover my erection with my shirttail.

"It's like," she said, "he's been replaced by someone I don't love."

"It's going to be okay. I'll keep an eye on him."

We sat together like that until we heard the TV turn off. Mrs. Pickens rose quickly and trotted out of the room. She stood in the entry, smiled at me through smudgy eyes, and I stared for a silent moment at my muse. I poked out my chest and aimed my chin at her with a new sense of purpose as she opened the door for me. I tipped my imaginary hat and left.

Out in the night air I felt like a man of experience. I needed only take what I wanted, anything and everything.

A month later Suede called at ten till midnight. Calls after nine-thirty made my stepdad spitting mad. I begged him to take his two cents and get off the phone.

"What is it?"

"Vagina," Suede whispered.

The bewilderedness in his voice was proof enough. He was so many light-years ahead of us then. Until very recently, for the bulk of my short life, I'd assumed the female netherworld was U-shaped.

"So how do you feel?"

"Pickled," Suede said.

"Is that good?"

"I think so."

I sat back aghast in my beanbag, astounded he could speak after such an event. How could he go on with life so upended?

What was left to conquer? What was left to destroy?

In a dream I conjured Cindy Pickens in a field of fire and lilies.
She wore her apron and a frilly blouse before her clothes popped
off like bubbles. Naked, she was Shannon Tweed, Queen of
Cinemax. Her skin frothed and spat with heat. She touched me
and I woke up seething, convulsing. I gasped at the darkness above
my bed while her burning image floated close, her net of auburn
hair enmeshing us.

The next morning my mother caught me cramming my sheets
into the washing machine. I wrestled them away from her. Finally,
she saw the horror in my eyes and understood.

"I'm sorry," she said. "I forget how grown up you are now."

Mortified, I kept turning the knob on the machine. *CLICK,
CLICK, SWOOSH. CLICK, CLICK, SWOOSH.* Shame made me
insane and stupid. My hands were like paddles.

"You're growing up so fast," she said.

She calmly turned the dial to the correct setting and tried to
touch my cheek—I batted her hand away. Her eyes filled with hurt.

The tail of her housecoat followed her out of the laundry
room. The machine hummed, twisted, and vibrated. I couldn't wait
to escape that house of guilt and mediocrity. I made sure Mother
couldn't hear me crying in there.

Junior year, Suede's last soccer game became infamous. His events
were always well attended, but even his father was in the stands for
this, with Walkman headphones and a new John Deere baseball
cap. Cindy, in her full glory, never appeared to look at anything
other than Suede.

I rode the bench for much of the game because some of the
guys had dared me to stuff the coach's filing cabinet with inflated

condoms. Becky Myrtletree sat in the stands, far from Suede's parents. She was with her own flock of disciples, a fantastic bevy of ebullience. Before the game Suede had said he didn't care who won.

"How much winning do we have to do?"

I nodded without comprehension. If I could relive that moment, I'd tell him what I learned from our many victories: you go on winning until there's no one left who can touch you.

In the first half, he scored two quick goals. Since most of the visiting team was guarding him, he kicked the ball to Chuck, another forward. Everyone on or around the field, including Chuck, gasped. It was such a risk when the crowd wanted a sure thing. Chuck was so shocked he kicked it back to our goalie, who was so surprised he tripped on his feet and the visitors scored.

In the second half Suede refused to play offense. He only played spectacular defense and passed the ball to our teammates, who were catching on to the whole teamwork aspect of the game. But the crowd had had enough. They booed and threw breath mints. Coach called time-out and gave Suede a talking to.

"You've got to score!" Coach frothed, his hands twisted into claws.

The referee blew his whistle. The ball came to Suede and he rushed down the field and booted it over the opposing goal and the red dirt hill behind. Coach took him out and put me in. No argument from Suede, but his father shouted and cursed his cheeks full of blood. Every time I looked at Suede, he was watching us, enjoying himself.

We won, but Suede's fans booed anyway. They didn't care what had changed in him. They didn't understand what I'd tried to grasp, the philosophy and poetry of Suede. They wanted another massacre.

Afterward, his parents shooed him into the back of their

Yukon. I saw the look on Cindy's face before she climbed in the passenger side. It was like her son had dropped dead on that field.

The next day the school smeared us with gossip. Suede went crazy, they said. Crystal meth, cocaine, and acid. He'd whipped it into a cocktail and shot it in the vein. We heard that his folks sent him to one of those teen rehab facilities. They told Becky not to contact him anymore.

When he returned he was not our Suede. He slouched and smoked cigarettes in the parking lot with the Iron Maiden-shirt-wearers. In the neighborhood he ignored me, never looked my way. It felt like exile. I stared out my bedroom window at the highway roaring past Waterwood, the dandelion meadow where we'd buried Belch.

He grew his hair long and started a band that played primitive music in soiled garages: Suede and The Swedes. I saw the flyers and heard tongues wagging but cared only for Cindy.

Becky Myrtletree had begun dating Buck Simpson in Suede's absence. The entire school anticipated a rematch, but the calendar pages flipped without bloodshed. Simpson, back in the ascendancy, made threats, but only after he was sure he was in the clear. By the start of senior year, Suede had quit school and moved out of Waterwood to work at a gas station in Richland, a squalid backwater to our south.

One night not long after he moved, I knocked on Mrs. Pickens' door, hoping to catch a glimpse of the apron, the knee, the red lips or wringing hands. There was no answer. I knocked again, harder. The lights upstairs went out.

I wanted to tell her about my future rising like the morning star, the future I tasted like it sat on my tongue. I'd go to school and more school, learn the art of making money and turning women's heads. I'd grow my lip fuzz into a mustache. I'd have my own castle and cars, curio cabinets and grandfather clocks. If she had answered the door, I would've told her, "For you, I'll remake the world. I'll build happiness from nothing."

I stood on that lawn and stared up at the black windows until the sprinkler system engaged and wet me to the knees. I wasn't special. For every Suede, there were billions like me making do with what floated in the wake.

I scuttled back home.

A few weeks before graduation, Suede and The Swedes played The Black Wall, an old train depot converted into an all-ages venue. I climbed through a cloud of smokers to pay the door charge, got my hand stamped with a smiley face. There he was, Spawn of Cindy, onstage and shouting into a microphone while sweaty degenerates down front mashed against each other.

I stood in back to watch him prowl and loom over the crowd like an acrobatic Svengali. When the audience teetered on the edge of riot, he'd grab the nearest girl's hand and croon to her while the band downshifted from rock to roll. If the audience got bored, he'd scream and berate them until the band whipped back up full blast. He threw melted beer bucket water and the crowd cooed and licked. Everything he ever did on the field, the way he commanded attention and made us feel, he did it onstage for the rabble.

He leaned on a table afterward as kids mumbled up to shake his hand. The Swedes pushed around equipment and laughed at inside jokes. I waited my turn. Suede smirked at me.

"Hey," he said, "how's my mom doing?"

"I went by a while back but she wouldn't see me."

"Yeah, I know the feeling." He took a long swig from a water bottle. He looked ruddy and handsome under the lights, at home in the world in a way I'd never be. I finally realized I hated him.

"Listen," he said, "a few of us are going over to my buddy's place. It's an apartment on Old Canton Road. BYOB."

"I can't." I bit my cheeks. "Homework."

He nodded and cocked his head in a new way, like he recognized me from somewhere other than school and Waterwood. Like he knew each cell of me already and had lost interest. "That's a shame. Maybe next time."

We shook hands.

In the parking lot some thirteen-year-olds were shotgunning Colt 45 and smashing empty cans on their foreheads. One of them said, "Hey, you know Suede?"

"Yeah. Why?"

"Because he fucking sucks," the kid said. He high-fived his laughing friends.

I kicked that kid in the nuts.

The rest scattered into the bushes while I grabbed him, blacked out for a few seconds, and came to, snarling, "You don't know him! You don't know shit!" and pressing his face into the hood of a Datsun. When I let him go, the bum launched into the night, reappearing under the farther streetlights.

My arms and chest flexed. My mind was bleached with rage.

I felt ten feet tall.

I learned things in college about finance and women. After two years, I had a mustache and a few conquests under my belt, though I still thought of that night with Cindy on the couch, her naked knee.

On Christmas break, I went to Northpark, the shiniest mall in the land, to buy my mother a scented candle. I wandered out swinging the bag where the broad corridors intersected and dullards sat on uncomfortable benches spackling their faces with sugar.

                                                        Max Hipp

That's where I saw Cindy Pickens shuffle out of a shoe store. She wore a shabby dress, years out of style. I'd never noticed her dim sense of fashion, not to mention how the years were hanging on her neck skin.

Standing on the gleaming marble tiles, in the midst of seasonal commerce and all of humanity streaming past, I was transfixed. My heart had been so drunk, it made me question my judgments about Cindy and Suede. The last I'd heard, Suede and The Swedes had made an album and gone touring in an ancient station wagon. In my mind, he was still years ahead of me, but what if he'd fled someplace I never wanted to be, like prison or New Jersey? I steeled myself to ask about him as she approached. When she saw me, I imagined she'd grasp my hand, grateful and chatty. We could catch up by the fountain of lucky pennies. Perhaps she'd say, "I'm divorced," and offer a breathless, "I've been thinking of you."

She stared through me instead, no recognition, with a look of befuddled desperation, like the newly blind groping for the light switch. A chill of December air conditioning blew out of the jewelry store as she rounded the corner.

It was just as well. I vowed, right then and there, to never again let anyone get so close.

Farewell, my grail.

THE TIM DIET

Laramie is sitting at the window waiting for Tim to come home. She hopes they'll go to the grocery store to get makings for spaghetti. Then she can get some Choc-a-doo muffins too and maybe have something to eat during the day other than Tim's Tuffy Bars. But if he's drunk it'll be Burger Barn again. Mostly, though, she just wants him to walk through the door with that longing he whips out like a laser pointer, his cold gray eyes trained on her as every thought flies out of her head.

Across the street, the neighbor Tim calls Miss Carroll is walking down the driveway again to check the mail. Her clothes are too big. It makes Laramie giggle to see a woman wear suspenders. Honking cars pass and she waves. It's not clear Miss Carroll understands even who she is, much less who's passing by in cars. For some reason, she has to look inside the mailbox before putting her hand in, which she does cautiously, like it's rocket surgery, hugging the junk mail and letters to her chest as she scuttles back into the house. Laramie wonders if they're the only two people on the street at home alone all day.

Behind the ancient end table, every piece of furniture a hand-me-down from Tim's dead grandmother, Laramie finds Maybelle's rubber chew toy. A shard of her heart stabs her guts.

Maybelle loved her immediately—she hadn't had a dog since she was small—but Maybelle didn't like Tim. Tim said he wouldn't have a dog, not even his grandmother's dog, growling at him in his own grandmother's house when he got up to pee in the night. She squeezes the toy and feels the scars from Maybelle's gnawing.

She shivers and lights a Slim Spirit to stop the shakes. Tim had caught her stuffing dresses into her purse at XOXO. He acted like some undercover mall cop at first, waiting until she made it through the broken metal detectors and into the mall to grab her by the elbow and pull her against him, smelling like milk chocolate and leather, his body hard as a door. If she didn't go with him right then, he said, the police would make her life difficult. Then, when he took her hand, she felt pieces of herself she'd always wanted to release float up into the cloudy atrium.

She's on her last cigarette when his Toyota runs the stop sign down the block. Something in the back of her throat makes her want to throw up—no time to do it before he comes through the door. There's only time to look hot for Tim. *You're not hot enough,* the shadow voice says, the one she mostly ignores. She wants Tim to want her because without his wanting there's no gravity. She might fly into space.

He walks in and slaps a colorful swarm of flyers and coupons on the coffee table. He's told Laramie he likes to get the mail so he knows when her mom's check comes because he doesn't trust her with money. He unbuttons his work shirt with the name tag on it. He lied about his felonies and experience on his application at the temp agency, so, for a month now, he's watched the clock and collected pay in an air-conditioned office, says it's the easiest con he's ever pulled.

"Laramie," he says, "where have you been today?"

"Nowhere. I didn't leave the house."

"Nowhere?"

"Like you said."

He grins, showing straight gleaming teeth. He's like an underwear model wandered into a toothpaste ad. He picks up an envelope and tears it open. "What if I don't believe you."

Tim's tone squeezes her lungs and electrifies her at the same time. "I don't ever lie to you."

"Prove it."

Her throat is dry. She's afraid she might lose her voice.

He saunters up close without touching her. Unzips his fly in her face.

At breakfast, there's nothing to eat. Even though he doesn't want her to have a job and she doesn't have to be anywhere in the morning, he makes her get up to brew coffee for his thermos. She sits at the table feeling her hip bones through the pajamas and flipping through *Hot Cars Magazine* without really looking at it. She's grown rail thin in the two months they've been together. In the bathroom mirror, she no longer recognizes the bony face. Like a hungrier girl has possessed her body.

"What are you going to do while I'm gone?"

Part of her longs to obey and another part feels him training her to be someone else. The easiest move is to give the answer he wants. "Sit here and think about sex," she says.

"Good girl. And what's the other thing, Laramie? What's my rule?"

"Don't go anywhere."

"How come?"

She rolls her eyes. "So I don't meet Mr. Wrong."

He tucks his shirt into his slacks. "That's right. Every guy but me is Mr. Wrong. Don't forget that. Ever."

Even after he leaves, she can feel his grip on her arms, his words in her ear, his morning breath steaming down her t-shirt. She wonders how Mr. Wrong's hands might feel on her thighs. Mr. Wrong's eyes are just like Tim's: always watching so she says the right things.

She feels empty whenever he leaves. Her heart beats in her ears, sometimes so fast she wishes it would just stop. They found her father behind the lawnmower in a row of freshly mown grass. She wonders about the calm that comes after your heart stops, when the blood ceases and life no longer clamps down like a vise.

She puts on her new bikini, a size smaller now, like she's grown up but shrinking at the same time. Moments like these, she loves the way her body has changed from the Tim diet. Sometimes when he's gone, though, she suspects something isn't right, like maybe he lies to her about where he goes. How would she know if he just puts on that long-sleeved button-down and drives straight to another woman's house? Maybe that's why he doesn't want her to go anywhere. It might have nothing to do with Mr. Wrong.

She pulls the shoebox from under the bed. It's full of many small things she's stolen. There's the belt buckle Tim's so proud of, a coiled brass rattlesnake that says Don't Mess With Texas he stole off a bull rider from Odessa. Gold plated pendants from a short stint working at the pawn shop. Marbles and wheat pennies and Kennedy half-dollars, along with lipsticks she'll never use. She likes the colors and names like Midnight Mashup, Celeb Sexy, and Black Stallion Returns. She digs out the necklace from Bryan, her ex. In one of Tim's drunken rages, he flung it into the ditch, but she found and hid it, a gold cross on a thin chain, the nicest gift anyone has ever given her. She piles it in her palm and closes her hand, warming the metal before placing it back in the box.

Laramie goes onto the back patio and lights a cigarette from the new pack. The yard is flat and hemmed in by a grayed wooden fence. Sometimes the filthy orange cat next door climbs on top and watches her. Laramie sees something white next to the fence—one of Maybelle's milk bones. Border collies are so high-maintenance, she couldn't get her sister to take her. When they dropped Maybelle at the pound, wearing the powder-blue bandana to match her eyes, Laramie couldn't stop crying.

She spreads the towel on the lounger. She has no idea why she bothers wearing a bathing suit. All of the neighbors are at work and no one can see into the backyard. Nothing looks down on her but empty blue. She unfastens the clasp behind her back and lies on her stomach. She puts *People Magazine* on the concrete and flips through it in the shade of the lounger.

While she's lying there, Tim texts a picture of his monster. He likes to send pictures of it in strange places and situations, an ongoing story of what Tim's penis does at work. This time his monster is wearing one of those water cooler paper cups like a too-big hat. She texts back kissy lips.

That's when the dark voice speaks from the other side of the fence. *You're a terrible person*, it says, sounding something like her father, maybe some of her exes. Like men who have seen her naked and peered into her soul. The men who see the bad she's capable of.

"Not true," she whispers.

Then why did you let your boyfriend die?

Tears tap the magazine pages. Bryan's dimpled face. She'd never loved him but couldn't bring herself to dump him because she felt safe for the first time. He was pronounced dead at ten-fifty-eight p.m. from the wreck, right when she might've been orgasming in Seth's bed, a realization her mind can't quite grasp, two events that, once connected, become impossible to bear.

The voice on the other side of the fence laughs. The tone changes like bad voice scramblers on true crime shows.

Where were you?

She hates how the voice always says horrible things when she's alone. She picks up the towel and *People Magazine* and goes inside.

Laramie's stomach feels like it's eating itself, but maybe this is what it takes, this is how beauty must suffer. She looks in the refrigerator at the beer and ketchup and leftover ranch from last week's chicken wings. She gets so lightheaded on the way to her cigarette pack she has to rest on the sofa arm. She lights one, filling her belly with smoke. Tim's rules make her angry. If Miss Carroll can go to her mailbox, then why can't she?

She opens the front door. The flowerbed is overgrown, and wasps have nested under the eaves and crouch on the soffits with still black wings. She can feel Tim's disapproval already, like a drop of bleach on her skin. But Tim isn't the one home all day with terrible thoughts, no food, and nothing to drink but water.

The walk down the driveway to the mailbox feels good. The sun is shining and it's not too hot yet. There's a letter for Miss Carroll that the mailman has misboxed. Laramie looks back at Tim's house from the edge of the driveway, the overgrown hedges and thin, off-white curtains. It feels like Tim's lurking behind them, watching her disobey.

Disobeying gives her strange new energy. She crosses the street with Miss Carroll's letter from the city and knocks on the door and stands on the porch in her bathing suit for what feels like forever, a few honkers slowing down as they pass.

Miss Carroll opens the door and spreads her arms wide. "Tillie! I didn't know you were coming!" Tears of happiness in her eyes. "Come in! Come in!"

The right thing is to tell her she's not Tillie, but she's so enthusiastic, Laramie might want to be Tillie. She walks in and gives Miss Carroll, who smells like baby powder and livestock, a big hug. She scans the room for valuables, nothing shiny in sight. The place is lined with stacks of newspapers and books. She can't see much of the wallpaper and can only walk the worn path in the carpet.

"I can't believe it!" Miss Carroll says. "Sit down. *Please* sit!"

Laramie sits on the couch as Miss Carroll drops into the ancient, cracked recliner and pulls the lever. An enormous mechanical *bong* resonates as she rocks back with a wide, closed-lipped smile.

"I'm so glad you came," she says. "I didn't think I'd ever see you again." Then her face goes slack and pale. "You were with that bastard. He killed you." Her mouth tightens into a gnarled onion ring. "What I wouldn't give for five minutes alone with Harry."

Her bleary eyes light with something Laramie's never seen. It knocks fear out of her head and fills her chest with heat. "Well, I've got your letter. The mailman sent it to the wrong house." She places it on the coffee table.

"It'll be fine, hon," she says, waving it off. "Tell me how you've been. Tell it straight, baby. You can't get anything past me. I know the way Harry treats you."

"He's not all bad." Laramie pictures Tim's toothy smile, the one that melts her. "Sometimes he's pretty good."

Miss Carroll looks through her for a moment, like she's thinking about bombs going off and tanks crushing skulls. "He killed you, baby," she whispers through gritted teeth. "He killed you."

Laramie doesn't know why—maybe it's the Vick's VapoRub in the air that reminds her of her grandmother—but something in her tears open and she's sobbing, grossing herself out with snorting noises. She remembers her mother, always waving goodbye. "I just want someone to love me," she squeaks through the snot.

"Tillie," Miss Carroll says, "Harry doesn't love anyone but himself."

Sometimes Laramie believes she's cursed to never have love with anyone because she's done horrible things and maybe she and Tim aren't so good together. Probably the best thing to do is walk to the bus stop and sayonara. Her lungs seal with snot. She's almost hyperventilating by the time she looks at Miss Carroll again.

"It's okay, hon," she says. "Mama loves you so much. Mama loves her little pumpkin patch. Don't you forget."

Laramie takes Miss Carroll's hand and squeezes it. Soon she's taking deeper breaths.

She wants to thank her, so when she goes in the kitchen for some water and sees the sink full of dirty dishes and the over-flowing trashcan, she starts tidying up. The sponge is dry but she resurrects it with dish soap, scrubs the plates and forks until they're crud free. Soon the sink is empty enough to wipe some of the rust rings at the bottom.

A new pack of cookies sits on the counter. She sneaks five or six, feels slightly guilty, and sneaks a few more. That's when she spies, buried behind stacks of legal pads and loose papers, the collection of silver spoons in a shadowbox on the wall. In her grip, they're heavy as lead.

It's getting late, though. Almost Tim time.

When she returns to the living room, Miss Carroll looks asleep. Laramie tries to sneak by, but she springs out of the chair and smiles, shows her capped teeth.

"Do me a favor." She grasps her shoulder. "Get away from Harry. He's no good, pumpkin."

Miss Carroll won't let go until she promises.

That night Tim takes her to Wanda Beef, where she orders three

                          Max Hipp

items off the Cheapo Menu: Baby Cheeseburger, Baby Fries, and a Shakey.

He glares. "Shakies are nothing but fat."

By the time they put the food on the tray, she's nauseated and can't eat. He eats his food and then hers. His nostrils flare. He sticks out his lower lip. "Suck it up, Buttercup."

"Why are you so mean?"

He repeats her words in the key of asshole.

She remembers Miss Carroll's smooth hands, how nice she was, how it felt to leave the house today. Tim's expression, mixed with the meanness, feels like bricks stacked on her windpipe. It makes her want to change the look on his face.

"I know something you don't know," she blurts.

The grin goes away but his teeth don't. "You only know what I tell you, Laramie. So, by definition, you couldn't possibly know something I don't. That's not who you are. You're not the kind of person who knows things I don't know." Whenever he wants to point out how dumb she is, the words *by definition* show up.

She tells him about Miss Carroll, a little senile and slow, but nice. She tells him Miss Carroll thinks she's her dead daughter come back to life, how her house is filled with newspapers and catalogues, how the kitchen is filled with too many dishes, knickknacks, wadded paper towels, reams of paper, and utensils. She tells him the news he'll love: that she stole her silver spoons, and the best part is she'll never notice. But he doesn't seem to care what she stole. He gets this look on his face like he's hearing not only her words but someone else's too. His left eye starts twitching the way it does when the Dallas Cowboys lose. By the time she's done telling him, she feels better. It feels good to tell the truth. Secrets take so much out of her.

"You're not mad?

He laughs. "Now, Buttercup, why would I be mad at you?"

The next day she's sore and trying not to limp. There are bruises on her neck and she does neck stretches in the bathroom mirror. He was rougher than ever, left her crying with her wrists zip-tied too tight while he played video games.

She makes coffee because she doesn't want him any angrier. She hates coffee so much.

"Guess what?" he says. "Since you're so good at lying and acting, you're going back over to Miss Carroll's place to do the poor dead daughter routine again." His tone is like he's her know-it-all teacher. "Like you did yesterday when I thought you were home waiting for me. The difference is, when she falls asleep this time, you find where she keeps her money. Or maybe you find her social security checks, her jewelry upstairs. Whatever she's got."

Laramie stares at the woodgrain in the table and thinks of Miss Carroll's cookies, how she was kind and caring even when she ugly-cried.

He flexes his chest like he's deciding what to do with her next. "You are to do this by the time I get home from work. You hear me?"

She nods.

"I don't want to get nasty with you. Because if you think last night was nasty, you're dreaming. I'll make you wish for another night like last night."

He puts his hand on her head and smiles like he means this to be romantic, like she wants to be tied to the bed for hours while he does what he wants to her and plays video games. She forces herself to smile back.

"Good," he says. "I'm glad we agree."

Out in the backyard she's got the same suit on, the magazine, the towel. Still no orange cat. She lies in the sun with the lounger pointed in the same direction, but it feels like she's in the wrong yard, behind the wrong house.

Tim texts another picture of his monster. This time he's draped a necklace of green paperclips around it. She doesn't feel anything for the picture but sad before she texts back kissy lips. He asks if she's hanging with Miss Carroll. She tells him not yet.

"Obey."

She stares at the word and wonders how she gets into these relationships. Always someone telling her what to do, what not to do. It feels good at first. Then not so great.

It's because you're crazy, says the voice from the other side of the fence. *You've never been faithful to anyone in your life.*

"You never once asked me anything about me. You don't know where my sister lives or how many times we've seen *Forty Weddings*." The voice doesn't know that when Jaws got hit by a truck, her father tucked him in his dog bed so Laramie could say goodbye.

Bryan drove around looking for you. Got smeared in the road like ketchup and fries.

"I didn't kill him," she says, her eyes tightening. "It was an eighteen-wheeler."

The voice from the other side goes silent. It's never let her get the last word before. Maybe the voice is wrong. Mr. Wrong.

She texts, "I'm going over this afternoon."

Tim sends a smiley face, a thumbs-up.

She goes inside and picks up Maybelle's chew toy from where she's hidden it under the couch. She squeezes it until she can breathe again.

She puts on jeans and a t-shirt and digs in the closet for her woven purse to hold Miss Carroll's loot and walks across the street with it hanging from her shoulder, empty except for the chew toy.

Miss Carroll opens the door wide and points a pistol at her. "Who the fuck are *you*?" she says, eyes narrowed, jaw tensed. Like a madwoman has answered the door.

"Your neighbor," Laramie says, pointing. "From across the street?"

"Never seen you before." She glares. "What do you want?"

Laramie falls to her knees on the porch. The Tim diet is too much. Worrying about Mr. Wrong is too much. She can't rob Miss Carroll of anything anymore, not even junk.

"Hey, hippie girl," she says, grabbing her, resting the butt of the pistol on her shoulder, "the hell's the matter with you?" Laramie sobs and Miss Carroll tucks the pistol into her belt. "Get in here," she says, looking at the street. "I don't want anybody I know riding by to see this shit."

She hushes her inside and plants her on the couch. It takes a while, but she finds a box of tissues and a cup of water. When Laramie asks for chocolate chip cookies, she drops the same bag on the table, sits in the recliner without hitting the lever this time. Laramie starts devouring the cookies, notices Miss Carroll watching, and chews more slowly.

"I used to be a detective," she says. "I might be retired, but I'm sharp enough to see somebody falling apart."

Laramie feels stupid crying in front her. "I'm so sorry about this."

"Can the apology. Just tell me what's wrong."

The voice from the other side of the fence says, *Tell her you're crazy. Tell her nobody in this world will ever love you.*

"I don't know," she says. "I don't know what's wrong."

Miss Carroll stares at her, reminding Laramie of a falcon she once saw at the zoo, how its gaze hooked into her cheekbones. After a moment or two, she turns on the Western channel. Black-and-white cowboys ride through gray canyons. Laramie eats the cookies, imagining Maybelle weaving through the horse legs. She piles snotted Kleenex on the floor and stares at the brown furniture and brown curtains and fake paneling. She sinks into the cushions, tonguing the cookie muck in her teeth, her eyes puffed and heavy, feeling surrounded by smells and soft sounds like her grandparents' house before everybody started dying off.

"You're a strange girl," Miss Carroll says.

You got that right, says the voice.

She wakes, startled, to Tim coming through the door. He glares murderously while Miss Carroll sleeps in the recliner. He puts a finger to his lips and creeps toward the stairs but starts laughing and has to shush himself because he's drunk. Laramie shakes her head. He gives her the bird and goes up. He stumbles around upstairs, trying to be quiet.

Miss Carroll wakes up. "Tillie," she says. "You're back."

"That's right." Laramie's hand slides into the purse, grips the chew toy. "I'm here."

Upstairs there's a loud crash. Tim hoots.

Miss Carroll raises an eyebrow. "Tillie," she says, licking her lips. "Is it Harry?"

Her nails dig into the toy's splits and punctures. "No, Mama," she says.

"Don't lie, hon." Miss Carroll seems to peer through the ceiling. "He's up there."

Another bumping sound above, a dresser drawer opening and closing. Miss Carroll searches for the pistol and can't find it. But she slides out the coffee table drawer and there's another one on a stack of yellowed coupons and flyers. She pulls it out like a long, silver dream.

"He's not getting away with it," Miss Carroll says.

She stands, holding the gun steady, two hands in front like a movie cop. Tim trudges like Miss Carroll is deaf. Laramie said she was old and slow, not deaf. Her phone dings and Miss Carroll stares a hole through her. It's another picture of Tim's monster, this time with a roll of Miss Carroll's greenbacks rubberbanded to it.

Laramie texts back thumbs up. Kissy lips.

Rotten, nasty. This time the voice sounds like Tim. But she knows how Mr. Wrong Tim can be.

When he stomps across the landing and the stairs start creaking under his weight, Miss Carroll hardens into a shooting stance against a tower of magazines. Laramie covers her mouth, her eyes wide and watching Tim appear from the darkness like a bad dream in slow motion. His feet and ankles, then his knees. Miss Carroll aims. Laramie waits for his eyes. She wants him to see the expression on her face, the one that says I know something you don't. You wouldn't believe the things I know.

BLACK BALLOONS

Wake to the sound of the TV switching on in the living room. The volume swells with some infomercial about sharp knives. You think it's Beth until she sits up straight as a yardstick in the light through the blue curtain and clutches her housecoat collar.

"Is somebody out there?"

"TV's screwed up," you say. "The buttons are stuck." You bought it on sale, probably made by somebody living in a Chinese factory.

The channels change from *Mr. Ed* to the terrible people always arguing on reality TV. You suspect there's a school that trains them to be hateful for cameras. You're putting on your slippers to go out and shut it off when there's this plaintive whine followed by a booming, wet sneeze.

"Oh, Arnie!"

Before Beth can say another word, reach for the cold butt of the Glock on the nightstand and unsnap it from the holster. Put one in the chamber and hold it to your chest.

"I'm going to take care of it," you say.

"You're not going out there!" Her whisper is louder than her normal voice. "It could be a whole gang!" Something about her fear calms you. You went to war on a godless continent, after all, and returned. Compared to that, this is nothing.

Hold her by the shoulder. "I'm going to lock this door behind me. I want you to put the chair against it and call the police. If anyone tries the door, open the window and go to the Crawfords'."

"This is a terrible idea."

Think if she were herself right now, she'd be sensible. "Go ahead and call the police. Please, Beth."

She groans and starts dialing. "If you get yourself killed on my new carpet, I'll never forgive you, Arnie Washington."

Forty years of marriage comes down to carpeting. Wood floors in the dining room, but she needed low pile in the living room. Huey, your one fully mobile and useful friend, helped you install the kitchen cabinets. Kirk, your son, only proves himself more useless as he gets older. Remember the teenage years of sullen looks, emotional outbursts, and resentments. He lives on the left coast, surrounded by activists and people scamming for government handouts. It raises your blood pressure.

Beth says, "Mercy," as you close the door and lock it.

The flashing TV lights the hallway. Its speakers rattle a nature show, birds chirping and screeching.

Palm the drywall and exhale through clenched teeth. Peek around the corner. On the couch sits a boy with his feet on the coffee table, blond hair like Kirk's in kindergarten, before it darkened along with his attitude. The boy leans back with his mouth open, hands on his kneecaps like he's had a long day. No weapons on the couch or on the coffee table. His t-shirt and shorts fit tightly, nowhere to hide anything. The kid looks half-asleep, and wet, like he's crawled through the creek behind the house.

If this boy comes at you, can you accept the consequences, put your faith in the higher power to protect your wife and home? Yes, you can. Sometimes men are called to defend what's theirs.

Step into the room with the Glock trained on him. He places a cigarette behind his ear as you approach. Onscreen, a flock of geese flies over a winter lake. There's a pungent smell, like a garage with an open drum of gasoline. He must've spilled gas all over himself somehow, probably tracked it across Beth's carpet. In this transgression, you feel connected to the boy, who, in his gauntness, reminds you of those you served with who never made it home. A boy on a minefield road, like your son. He could've walked out of grainy footage of blown rice paddies from fifty years ago.

Sit in the recliner and pick up the remote without taking your aim off him. Press the volume down. Reach across your body to the lamp. Squint against the explosion of light.

Lines on his face. Not a boy at all but a man in his forties, arms lined with tattoos of dragons, stars, demons—you can't see what all swims up the man's shirt. People love tattoos now, whole bodies covered in monsters. Even Kirk.

"So," you say. "Who are *you?*"

The man's face angles at you. His eyes seem to skip.

"Do you know where you are?"

No telling what drugs have done this. Something that peps you up and drives you out of your mind, into a stranger's house. The brains of the youth are wired wrong these days. You've stopped having political conversations with Kirk on the phone. It crosses your mind that perhaps you raised Kirk badly, but the idea quickly scuds away; even if that were true, anyone worth his salt has ample opportunity to overcome and succeed in this country.

"I went to the Grand Canyon," the man says.

"You did? When was that?"

"The ravens." He leans forward. "They're the size of two crows." The gasoline stench shoots up your nose like an acrid needle.

"Son," you say, "was there some kind of accident?" Something might've happened on the road that knocked him delirious.

"Ravens float over the nothing over the canyon like black balloons. Risen spirits."

"Are you a spiritual man?"

He stops blinking for a moment. "Yes, sir." He removes the cigarette from behind his ear to hang it between his lips.

Relax slightly. Aim the Glock toward the man's side rather than his center. Better a Christian believer breaks in than someone who believes in nothing, like Kirk. This could be a turning point in the man's life, a moment like Saul's on the road to Jerusalem. God sends messengers. Perhaps God meant this guest to learn something.

"Beth!" you shout. "Are the police on the way?"

The bedroom door rattles with unlocking.

"Yes," she calls. "Everything okay?"

"Stay where you are. Everything's going to be fine."

The guest remains calm despite his darting eyes.

Congratulate yourself on not shooting. Imagine the parade of policemen and detectives, questions and paperwork—a crime scene in Beth's house. Most men would shoot first, and by law they'd have the right, but there are men's laws and the laws of Jesus. Jesus appears in your mind in a brilliant white smock, attending boil-ridden lepers. Jesus wouldn't shoot an uninvited guest. It's not the Lord, though, but you who'll have to fix busted windows.

Your mood darkens. It happens more and more now in your seventies. Remember taking Kirk to see fireworks the first time. A quilt pitched on the courthouse lawn. Beth brought a picnic basket with roast beef and mustard sandwiches, the July evening humid and clear. But when the fireworks began, Kirk cried and screamed his head off for his stuffed animals.

"Listen," you say, your jaw tightening. "Do you know how

close I came to shooting you?" Tracked-in mud maybe and shat-
tered glass. You'll have to steam-clean the carpet and couch. "How'd
you get in here? Which door?"

The guest cocks his head and stares at you. "I camped on the
canyon floor. It gets cold down there at night."

"Did you hear what I said, son?" Rise out of the chair and
try to glimpse any forced entry in the kitchen, then regain your
position and keep the gun on him.

"Bottom of the world in the belly of the beast. Imagine the
stars at the bottom of the world."

It slips your mind sometimes, when you wake in the middle of
the night, but it hits you now like a cinderblock to the chest: Kirk
will be gone a year this April. Shot in Seattle over nothing. The
heaviness of his death sinks inside you. You can't imagine stars over
the canyon. Or anywhere else.

"I got cold." The guest stares at the TV as if staring into *cold*.
"Scrounged for kindling."

Try to breathe. Strain to hear sirens in the distance, any *blips*
and *whoops* blasting against the night. Instead there's a clicking
sound and the waft of gasoline hits you again, like the wind has
shifted, the AC coming on.

"Need an accelerant to start fires," the guest says. He brings
the lighter out and puts it to the cigarette.

Another *click*.

Hold the gun in front of your face, against the rush of flame
summoned from the air, the moment bearing down like you've
overcorrected while driving and scenery is whipping by on all
sides, not trees and highway signs blurring but the furniture of
your living room. You're struck by a groping clairvoyance. Your
small town will recount the story of the man who drank gasoline
from the pump and broke into your house, like a cautionary tale.

Questions will follow. What in hell were you thinking, carrying out such shenanigans? You face your accusers in that speculative future: *He seemed a lost boy in a broken world, no different than Adam who took the fruit. I chose to be Christlike. Would I again? Would I do it differently, Kirk, with your mother clambering out the window in her nightgown, the framed pictures of our lives catching fire?*

A great *whoosh* singes your eyebrows. Army-crawl toward the front door. Incendiary devices ignite again in a jungle of menace, the ordnance so close, for a flashing moment, the dead seem to commune once more with the living.

WHAT DOESN'T KILL YOU OPENS YOUR HEART

TO THE FACTORY, COLLEGE BOY!

In the gravel lot, I decided I deserved this. Southern Baptist God, SBG for short, had willed it. The cabinet factory backed up to the woods, the last industrial park lot off County Road 101, a sheet metal building the size of an airplane hangar. I was on the edge of town to fill out an application for a job I didn't want, a lead from the old man.

This was back in 2000. I'd just graduated with an English degree and (surprise!) wasn't making any money. I was ignorant enough to believe I could be a writer, that someone would want to read my stories. To top it off, I couldn't tell a story to save my life.

Under the high yellow lights, men stooped behind sanders and saws. Sawdust hung in the air above the screaming blades. The factory hissed *kill, kill, kill,* like all inventions of mankind.

I ducked into the office where a big desk spattered with files, clipboards, dirty mugs, catalogs, and tape measures loomed under a dim fluorescent bulb. I must've looked crazy when Petty came in.

"Good god," he said, "what's the matter?"

I asked for the application. He opened a drawer, rummaged, passed the form, and left me to fill it out. It was redundant and meaningless, like all applications. When he didn't come back, I tossed it on the desk pile and walked out expecting nothing.

He called the next day to tell me I had the Cabinets Limited job.

"But you've got that college degree," he said. "How do I know you won't get bored and leave?"

"Because of the landlord and the bills."

"I hear that," he said.

And hot damn, the next day I was a fucking carpenter.

THE COTTONMOUTH

I liked to ride with Hardy Null around the long curves of Old Sardis Road. She liked it on picnic tables the most and there were some good concrete-topped ones out at Sardis Lake.

I'd see her between girlfriends, or sometimes during girlfriends, like there was a tractor beam between her legs. She handled my penis with heroic resolve. But if I ever meet her father I will knock teeth down his throat for naming her so ugly.

One night at the lake, we were going at it with her on the table, the backs of her knees on my shoulders, my shorts and underwear around my ankles. I stopped when I felt something bump my shoes.

"What's wrong?" she said, annoyed.

The last half of a cottonmouth slunk over my shoelaces. Not as vicious as people claim, but not to be fucked with.

                                                        Max Hipp

"Snake," I said. "Big one."

It was an omen. Good or bad, I didn't know.

Hardy reached down and started slapping me between the legs, gently, as if waking a favorite pet.

LETTER OF INTENT

I wrote my letter to get into the University of Mississippi's Master of Fine Arts program. They'd just started it and seemed to be letting in almost anyone. My one reader-writer friend, who was already in the MFA program, told me I'd need to describe my intentions and why I wanted to be in graduate school in the first place.

I started with the truth.

Dear Faculty:

Books weren't part of my childhood. I didn't grow up wanting to be a writer. I wanted to be a pilot, a center-fielder, or a soldier like Rambo. I wanted to play guitar like my father Benton Meeks but didn't have the discipline to practice.

I got to college and discovered literature was music made of words. James Joyce's Ulysses *lit me up—some white-haired saint taught the class. I said, "I can do this." Yeah, right.*

Then I slanted it different.

Dear Faculty:

I want to go to your school because I don't know what to do with my life. Currently, I work forty hours a week in a cabinet factory, the only decent paying job I was able to find in town with a bachelor's degree. I'm hoping with a master's

to get the fuck out of here and start paying off student loans.
I'm scared shitless and don't know what else to do.

Seemed a good start. But I needed to establish my qualifications.

I published a story in Blood River *called "Wild*
Dead Girl." The editor there called it "fucking awesome." I
haven't been writing all my life, like most applicants to your
program. Reading was always hard for me due to laziness.
But the more I read and write, the more I want to, and I'd
like to keep reading and writing in graduate school.

Sincerely,
Clay Meeks

PS: Some money would be nice. And a blow job.

BIRTHDAY

Benton Meeks barely fit on the barstool, smelling like Barbasol and WD-40, his eyes blue as hell like mine. I slapped him on the back and sat down.

He told the bartender it was my birthday. Twenty-three. The bartender uncrossed his tattooed forearms, poured us tall shots and said, "Those are on me." He'd just been loitering before, but now he was angelic, godlike.

Daddy pushed both shots to me and held up his beer. "Here's to life," he said, "the best gig in town."

With that, cheap whiskey burned a trail down my esophagus. Twice.

He told me his next show was a dive close to the Tunica

                                                    Max Hipp

casinos that paid out of the bar whether anyone showed up or not. He rode those highways late at night, beer in cup-holder, cooler on the front seat, guitar and amp behind him, still playing a young man's game.

We wolfed down steak wraps and drank a few pints. He wasn't telling my birth story. He normally told it every year like it was occurring to him for the first time. I was starting to feel cheated, so I prompted him. He raised his beer and cleared his throat.

"You're born pissing," he said. "You piss all over the doctor and me and your mother. The floor, the bed, the machines. Your little dick whips back and forth," he wagged his finger in the air to demonstrate. "The doctor says it means you're healthy."

We ordered another round. He leaned on his elbow. A television mounted in the corner above the bar flashed baseball highlights.

"Your mother sure is proud of you," he said. "Wherever she is."

He was terrible to Mary Lou, my mother. He ran around on her and some nights I'd hear her screaming at him. One Friday, when I was twelve, she didn't come home from work. The suitcase was gone, along with her best clothes. The old man found the car at the law firm with the keys fanned in the seat. After a week she sent a postcard from Boulder, Colorado announcing she'd run off with the son of the lawyer she worked for, James Willard Snell Jr. I suppose Snell Sr. drew up divorce papers and Benton just signed them.

She sent me birthday cards, called me when she could. She worked at a restaurant and said she'd never seen anything more beautiful than the Rockies. I'd imagine snowflakes falling on her shoulders when she took smoke breaks at an all-night diner where she wiped tables and handed out napkins, silverware, and straws to skiing tourists for piss-ant tips. The plan was to take a bus to see her one day, my first trip west. But her cards and calls stopped coming. I didn't ask Benton about it, figured she was finished with us, something I'd done or said, and it ripped me up inside. I tried my best to forget what was missing. After I turned sixteen, he told me she'd been driving to work and got t-boned at an intersection.

I slid one shot glass to the bartender, who refilled and slid it back. I held it up to toast.

"We're alive," I said. "They haven't taken that away yet."

"They can't kill us," Daddy said.

We drank to that.

AUDREY MOSS

I haunted the record store at Tupelo Mall, bought *Rain Dogs* on CD. Later, I found myself standing in line at the Häagen-Dazs. This woman fumbled through her purse for exact change and glanced back at me sloe-eyed, managing to smile warmly even when stressed. Her little girl stood beside her, pulling at the wonky bow in her hair.

When I stepped forward and slapped sixty-three cents on the counter, she beamed at me like I'd dragged her drowning body to the bank and pounded the water out of her.

We sat at a glass table in the middle of the mall and ate ice cream. Audrey Moss was a nurse. Her daughter was sweet Caitlin. I was the famous carpenter-cum-writer Clay Meeks.

That night she marinated steaks with Worcestershire, salt, pepper, and garlic in a Ziploc. We played Blondie on the turntable. Almost nobody had a turntable in those days. I held Caitlin's hands and she stood on my shoes and danced with me. We grilled and sat outside watching the good light fade, the air cooling like a blessing. Audrey squeezed Caitlin in her arms and spoke to her so sweetly, I realized she was a better person than I'd ever be.

                                                Max Hipp

After dinner I helped tuck Caitlin in. Later we put on VHS tapes from Audrey's porn collection, reenacted a few scenes, didn't stop until the next morning, almost time for her hospital shift.

While she showered, I made Caitlin a peanut-butter-and-jelly sandwich and a thermos of milk and held her hand by the mailbox until the bus came.

Audrey stood in the doorway in scrubs. "I've never felt anything like this," she said, her face still aglow. I kissed her like I believed it.

She beamed through the windshield as she pulled out of the driveway.

I pissed in the flowerbed like a raw young animal. Her empty comfortable bed called to me, but I locked her door and got in my truck anyway.

PETTY

The world outside fried in the sun, but the bathrooms were attached to the office and, by god, air conditioning, when there was none on the factory floor.

Petty was waiting for me when I came out, his sleeves rolled tight on his fat arms. He dyed his hair jet-black and sweated obscenely. I did my work and had half a brain, so he seemed to respect me. But his demeanor was dulled by years of following orders without question.

"We don't pay you to sleep in there," he said.

I opened the bathroom and let my stench float out.

He blinked once, undaunted.

"Don't make it a habit," he said.

"Don't make what a habit? Shitting?"

He walked off like a big shot and oozed back into the

air-conditioned office.

Life was full of people like Petty, pecking and gnashing and clawing. Sent from hell to stand in my way.

SIN D PORNO

With paycheck in pocket, I walked to Two Stick, the lone sushi bar in town. At the time, raw fish in seaweed paper and rice was the strangest thing anyone in Oxford, Mississippi had ever heard of.

It was after ten and the kitchen had stopped serving. A gaggle of waitresses scowled from a candlelit table. I'd once done one of them wrong so they all hated me. I'd really turned on the charm, though I'd never lied or made any promises.

A blond sat at the bar, wearing heavy black eyeliner and an oversized Iron Maiden t-shirt with the sleeves cut off so I could see her pit stubble. She had veiny arms and was kind of plain, but I could tell by the way she sat on the stool, her shoulders squared and the small of her back scooped, a strong tight body lurked under her clothes.

"Mind if I sit?"

She ashed her cigarette. "It's a free country sometimes."

The bartender, bless him, slipped me a High Life without my asking.

The blond eyed me coolly, asked what kind of music I liked. I named some well-known rock bands. She shook her head. "You like all that because it's been pushed down your throat."

"And you don't like it?"

"That's not what I'm saying. I'm saying I like independent rock and roll. American music."

"Like what?"

"Stick around and find out."

                                    Max Hipp

I took a swig and asked who the hell she was. Her band was called The Porno Sisters, which was play on The Pointer Sisters, a pun nobody ever understood. Her real name was Cindy Powell, stage name Sin D Porno. Her rhythm section was Hardcore Betty Porno and Jane Doe Porno. She pointed where they sat making out next to an enormous rubber plant in the corner. Guitar player Stiff Steve Porno was smoking weed in the van.

"I've got to change and round these bitches up," she said. "You staying?"

"I'm glued here," I said.

Fifteen minutes later they picked up their instruments and dashed into noise. They wore leather and spandex, real '80s shit. But listen to me when I tell you there is nothing sexier than a woman rocking out. My father saw Janis Joplin with Big Brother and the Holding Company in Austin, Texas. He was on acid, standing in a crowd of people, watching her quake and contort, and said he had a waking wet dream. Sin D had fastened her leather vest with a duct-tape X across the front. She spat Everclear onto a lit Bic—to hell with the fire code or anyone in the place— and fireballs bloomed from her lips. It was dangerous the way rock and roll is supposed to be. She was fearless and vital, while the band did tired, old Ramones Lite. There weren't many people there, but hell, our town was a notch in the Bible Belt.

In the finale Steve slung his guitar down and kicked the ride cymbal offstage. Jane Doe straddled Hardcore Betty on the drum stool and they made out with lots of hair mussing and flailing. Sin D jumped down and sat at the bar, sweat dripping from her earlobes.

All my arm hairs stood like lightning was about to hit.

"Goddamn, that was good," I said.

She snapped a match to a cigarette and mugged at the new

bartender, one of the waitresses who hated me, and asked for a beer.
I told the bartender I needed a beer too and to put Sin D's on my
tab. She ripped the caps off the beers and slammed them down on
the bar.

"For your information, asshole, the band gets free beer."
She walked away and pretended to take some pint glasses back
to the dishwasher.

Sin D leaned on her elbow, grinning. "You must be quite the
slimeball to catch that kind of venom."

"Everybody's got a fan or two."

She raised her bottle. I clacked mine against it.

The doorman stood over the moneybox, counting out a thin
stack of bills.

"I wish we had a few more bodies in here tonight. I don't think
we even covered our gas." Her voice was gritted with nicotine.
Dark roots showed in her hair. I should've ripped out my heart and
handed it to her, saved some time.

She said they were running The Buccaneer in Memphis,
Springwater in Nashville, The Nick in Birmingham, the
Chukker in Tuscaloosa, and back to Athens. Then she sighed
and rolled her eyes.

"Is that enough small talk for you?" She reached over and
unsnapped my pants.

"I was done ten minutes ago." I hopped off the stool. "I know
a place."

She followed me into the walk-in cooler. She was hot and
sweaty and flexible. To keep from blasting off too quick, I pictured
the Virgin Mary, which brought a kind of epiphany. With each
stroke, I left the world of strife and heartache and slipped into
sweet pockets of ecstasy, a feeling I wanted more than anything.

Somewhere in there the bartending waitress looked in, grabbed

                                                          Max Hipp

some beer, shut and locked the freezer. I knew where the emergency latch was, so I maintained each thrust like it was my last. We bumped against boxes of lettuce, stockpots of miso soup and avocado crates until I had my first internal orgasm, and we both screamed.

By sunup I was filling the Porno Sister van with gas and giving Sin D my number, drunk. Jane Doe and Hardcore Betty glowered at me, pig that I am. But, goddamn, wasn't it life we were living? Wasn't watching Sin D drive away suffering and bliss rolled into one? Isn't that how you know you're too warm yet for the grave?

I went home feeling invincible and didn't shower. Didn't want to wash her ocean scent off me.

ROAD TRIP

I returned to Tupelo, where Elvis and the buffalo roam.

Audrey wore a blue dress and had cut her hair to her shoulders. She tried to tell me things with her brown eyes. *Give me everything I need. Heal this pain.* She'd had a rough run already, marrying an abuser who left her and baby Caitlin, which filled my heart murderous. But for her own good, I considered ending our relationship. I wasn't who she needed me to be.

Still, there was the sex, and I wasn't sure anyone else besides her or Sin D could keep up with me. I wanted to help Caitlin and her mom just like I'd wanted to help The Porno Sisters. Maybe if I was a rich man I could solve everyone's problems, raise them up, keep everyone safe.

The flea market smelled like dust, exhaust, potpourri. Caitlin's shiny black plastic shoes clicked beside me. She wore a floral print Sunday school dress, string-bowed in back. I bought her a stuffed rabbit with mashed Milk Dud eyes. After that she hooked a finger through my belt loop. Audrey wrapped her arm around mine and leaned against me as we walked past each busy stall. We strolled the aisles gawking at awful antique furniture. I bought Lynyrd Skynyrd's *Gold & Platinum* LP for a dollar because it had "Coming Home," a song I didn't own. Daddy taught me to appreciate their tones and clean licks. Sometimes when I was alone, I'd sing along with Ronnie Van Zant and resurrect him from that plane crash in McComb.

The steak that night was good and rare. We watched a movie until Caitlin fell asleep, and we put her to bed.

Audrey was thirty-one. I knew I made her feel young and reckless again. She liked to sleep with her leg thrown on top of me, but I got hot and felt out of place like I did when I went to the Baptist church as a kid, all those people who looked down on me. I lifted her thigh off me and lay silent and still for a few minutes. I scooted a few inches and waited for her breathing to go back to normal before I moved again. Finally, I snatched my record from the side table, slipped down the stairs and out the front door, arriving home at three-thirty-seven a.m.

The phone rang as I was pulling the blanket to my chin. The music on the other end was loud and fast.

"Whatcha doing, slimeball?"

"Partying," I said. "What else?"

The music faded as she moved to a quieter room. "I'm at some asshole's apartment. He bought our album and says he wants to be our manager. Mostly, he wants to manage his way into my pants."

"I don't blame him."

"Well go ahead and give me some small talk. That way we can skip it when you come see me."

The New York Dolls' "Frankenstein" cranked up on her end. Someone passing near said something about tonsils.

                                              Max Hipp

"I want you this weekend," she said.

"Are you drunk?"

"Hell yes."

Technically it was Sunday. Athens was eight hours away. If I left right then, I'd get there at noon and would have to leave by eleven p.m. to make it to work at seven on Monday. I told her I'd call from the first payphone in Athens.

My brain pulsed with sugar and caffeine when Sin D pulled up at Citgo. She had on a Cure shirt, sleeves cut off, deep V collar, no bra, her eyes red with sleep deprivation. She tried to hand me some pills but they landed on what was left of a smeared hamburger. We went to her apartment and all we could do was pass out for a few hours.

At a party, we walked into a black room full of strobe lights. Everyone wore white corpse paint like it was Halloween. Jane Doe and Hardcore Betty had a piss bottle they were using to baptize the drunk and the passed-out-in-corners. Sin D wanted to dance, and when I say dance I mean jump up in the air and come down swinging your arms. I punched a hole in the ceiling and didn't feel it. I wondered if she'd been doing this her whole life or if she only did it for an audience, even an audience of one. She aimed her body like a missile.

Late in the night she dragged me into a dark closet. I perched on a vacuum cleaner, leaned against the wall and smelled the leather belts. She got silent like she'd passed out.

"I love you," she said, sounding sober when she wasn't.

"I know," I said, surprised.

Later, when I touched her in bed, I noticed the cigarette burns and cuts on the insides of her thighs.

"What's the worst pain you've felt?" she asked.

I told her about my mother leaving and all the years I thought she hated me, when she was just dead. I'd never told anyone before.

"Is that all you got?" she said. "Is that the worst?"

I asked about her life and she told me there were things she tried not to remember. A few minutes passed.

"I'd like to be something other than flesh," she said. "Light, maybe. Or rain."

She told me she liked me because I didn't try to tell her what to do. I almost proposed to her, but in my drunken state it occurred to me that marriage was just two people trying to control each other until one of them died. We ended the night exhausted, flanked by her two obese cats.

I got a couple hours' sleep and called the factory at seven. The receptionist put me through to Petty. I told him I was in Athens. There were a few seconds of silence and then a grumble in the affirmative. I was a good worker so he just said he'd see me the next day.

Her living room reeked of mold. There was a ceramic vagina full of spider eggs and ashes. Squirrel skulls lined the mantel over her bricked-in fireplace. We fucked and listened to records, sat around naked, fucked some more. She put on Subhumans, Dead Moon, Rudimentary Peni, Siouxsie and the Banshees, and Wire, great music I'd never heard that blew my mind. That afternoon of sight, sound, and touch sank into my gray matter.

Five hours later I was leaving. She wanted me to stay, and every time I tried to get in my car, she dug her fingernails into my arm.

Her cowboy boot bonged off my roof as I pulled into the road. I drove away slowly, watched her limp across my rearview mirror and pick it up.

Audrey had left seven messages on my machine since Sunday. The content ranged from "Where are you? What happened?" to a drunken Audrey calling me a "yellow-bellied motherfucker."

Then the messages veered back to "I'm sorry" and "I hope you're okay."

SPRAY ROOM

Before long, I'd learned how to run the panel saw and the router. I could drive the forklift, work the line, sand the doors and face frames, assemble drawers, finish the cabinets in quality control, wrap it all up in plastic and pack it into an eighteen-wheeler trailer. Every day I worked a different part of the line. Most people wanted to sand the doors or screw face-frames together from seven to three-thirty, do the same thing until they dropped.

The one place I would not be caught dead was the spray room. I worked there one day, sanding the finished cabinets with a sponge for a few hours with the women who did it every day. Even the young ones were thin and tired-looking. A dull haze hung in the air like maybe my contacts had glazed over from being in there too long. Everyone was supposed to wear dust masks. Petty would occasionally say something about it, but mostly he worried about loading the trucks and getting the orders out of the factory. It was so hot in the spray room, everyone kept their masks around their necks until they saw Petty coming and pulled them over their noses.

The women would come out of the spray booth, arms stained brown to the elbows, their faces sweaty from the respirator. The sanders came out rubbing their eyes. On my break, I wrote a story about Hardy Null working at the factory, going home at night, the brown stain running off her in the shower. Then I sat wondering when OSHA was going to ride in and do something about us.

POSTCARD

Sin D sent me a postcard from Dallas.

> *New lyrics. I sing them every night, pretending you're looking*
> *up at me.*

> *Crawl into my womb*
> *Be my baby/tomb*
> *Break me open wide*
> *I want you back inside*

I paced my kitchen, feet going *suck, suck, suck* on the linoleum.
I wanted to taste the fire blister on her lip, smell the smoke in her
hair. Stroke her pale, seething body.

Her words triggered a memory from when I was fifteen and
felt the cool downdraft of a summer thunderstorm blowing in
on my father's porch. The lightning boiled and the heavy clouds
made the world smaller. I prayed to SBG to give me someone or
something to kill or die for, the full bore of pain and pleasure. Hard
rain blew under the eaves and slapped the porch bricks, spattering
my feet and ankles. Something entered me that night. A restlessness
that keeps me hungry.

I wrote to Sin D about it and how I wanted her to have my
baby, how I wanted us to tear down every wall, but it turned into a
story where everything went wrong. The boy and the musician had
a baby and no money, no jobs. The boy robbed a cabinet factory. In
the end, he got shot by his own drunk mother.

It never made it to an envelope. But I slept fine knowing Sin

                                                          Max Hipp

D was out there, burning a hole with her deathray life.

NIGHTLIFE

Audrey put on her short green skirt and we went to The Swim.
She'd got a raise and her mother had Caitlin, so it was party time.
She took too many shots of tequila, some Buttery Nipples, and
knocked back a pink drink. It put this faraway-yet-determined look
in her eye.

"You're not as cool as you think you are," she said, pointing in
my face. "You've got some shit to figure out."

"You've got it all figured out?"

She closed her eyes tight and grinned.

She went to get us more drinks, planted her elbows on the
bar and started moving to the beat of whatever pop horror was
pumping through the stereo.

The girl standing next to her moved her boyfriend away and
glared. She leaned to Audrey's ear, said something, and leaned
back to take a swig of Budweiser. Audrey slapped the full beer
out of her mouth, exploding it on the floor. The girl tried to rip
off her own shirt like a wrestler, until her boyfriend stopped her
and everybody in the bar booed. She started screaming, her hair
messed, the left side of her face pink. She was redheaded and a lot
meaner than Audrey.

"You should quit while you're ahead on this one."

She wheeled on me. "You don't think I can handle this bitch?"

"You've already whipped her ass."

"I don't know," she said. "Might be fun."

I realized I loved her.

The bouncer tried to quiet the shrieking redhead. Audrey said,
"How bad do you want me right now?"

We left twenty bucks and full beers on the counter.

GRASSHOPPER

The buzzer went off above my head, rattling my teeth as I clocked in. Petty poked his big head out the office door. I waved. He popped it back inside.

I programmed the dimensions into the panel saw computer and had the big green machine cutting the birch in five minutes. I said what the hell and stacked the half-inch pine at six sheets instead of the usual four. I pushed the wood along the assembly line on the bald steel rollers, *clack-clack-clack*. While the machine ran, I read Larry Brown stories on the sly. I had the entire first order to the router by ten o'clock break and walked to the air hose and blew sawdust out of my leg hairs.

It was dead summer, July. The factory floor thermometer said ninety. I was getting tired of wasting time at the breaks. Most of us sat around in silence while the factory veterans talked. In the morning, everybody greeted each other or muttered to themselves or put their heads on the picnic tables. Afternoons, people talked about fishing, drinking, or cashing their checks.

I was at the break table, imagining Sin D and Audrey in erotic positions when Big Ollie walked up adjusting the waistband on his sweatpants. He measured and cut wood for the face frames.

"College boy," he said, smiling.

My end of the bench buckled toward him when he sat. One day, before I'd worked there, Big Ollie had cut the tops off his middle and index fingers while pushing wood through a table saw. He didn't even scream, just beat on Petty's door with his bloody fist and requested a ride to the hospital. They'd put his finger meat in a plastic bag of crushed ice, though it hadn't helped.

"College boy." He rubbed the back of his neck. "The fuck you doing in this place?"

"Making money."

"If had a college degree, they couldn't stop Big Ollie."

I told him I was trying to go back to school in January. His eyes widened. Everyone at the table was listening.

"College boy going back to school?" Then he let loose this deep bass laugh.

At that moment my hair moved slightly and I felt the pressure of something bouncing off my head. A grasshopper the size of a French fry landed on the Coke machine.

He pounded the table and said, "Something jumped off your head, didn't it?"

LET'S GO TO CHURCH!

I'd get off on Friday and head to Tupelo. We'd take Caitlin to movies and restaurants, or shop and picnic. I'd missed a lot of family time with Mary Lou leaving Benton, never feeling much togetherness. Audrey, Caitlin, and I did everything together except go to church. I told Audrey I'd had enough of church when I was a kid, knew all about SBG, didn't need it like she did.

One Sunday, she said, "Come on, Clay. Caitlin's been asking why you don't go."

"If you want me to," I said, "I'll tell her why."

She was in her bra and panties and gave me a stern look. She unhangered a dress and pulled it over her head. I felt the joy of great men through the centuries—Charlemagne, Abraham Lincoln, Martin Luther King—given the privilege of watching women dress and undress.

"She just thinks everyone loves Jesus." Audrey puckered for

lipstick in the mirror. "You're breaking her heart."

Her daddy had broken her heart when he ran off with the babysitter, and again last year when he decided to spend Christmas in Mobile with the babysitter's family. He'd sent Caitlin a card with a gift certificate to Wal-Mart. Her broken heart had nothing to do with me.

Audrey went downstairs. Before they left, Caitlin ran in and kissed me on the cheek.

QUALITY CONTROL

Some afternoons they put me in Mick's department at the end of the assembly line. He was pushing sixty and his arms were wiry and muscular. He'd been in the Navy but was really an old hippie who reminisced about his opium days.

Quality control's job was to hang doors, install drawers, and make sure the finish was on the correct side. We pushed cabinets along the rollers as we inspected them, putting hinges on the doors with air-powered screwdrivers. If the doors hung crooked, we bent the hinges until they looked right, and if a hinge broke in this process, we'd replace it; if the drawers didn't close flush with the face frame, we bent the drawer tracks and took out screws until they did. Some orders were done in a week, some took a month.

One afternoon when Mick was out, I worked quality control with Booty Munch. He had a shaved head and a meticulously trimmed goatee. The first few days I worked in the factory, I figured I was hearing wrong. They'd say to him, "What's goin' on, Booty?" and "Come over here, Booty Man."

The order came down the line. With our razor blades we cut cardboard off a giant spool and slap-stapled it to the unfinished sides of the cabinets before wrestling them off the assembly line and clustering them next to the loading dock.

	Max Hipp

I told Booty Munch a few superficial things about Sin D as we worked. He started talking about his girlfriend and stopped to pull a picture out of his wallet. A tall woman with curly weaves stood before a gray studio backdrop.

He smiled and said, "You know how to get your girl to really love you? So she never runs around?"

"Nope."

He looked me dead in the face. "Lick her asshole."

I winced. I'd never considered such.

"I mean," he said, "after she takes a good hot bath." He stood back and put his hands in the air, rolled his eyes back in his head. "She'll be like, 'OH! OH, DON'T STOP! DO IT! DO IT! UGH!'"

RETURN OF SIN D

She called from a pay phone to tell me to prepare myself.

The van pulled up at the sushi place at eight, already late for load-in. Sin D in ripped fishnets and black eyeliner. Jane Doe and Hardcore Betty had spiked their hair. Stiff Steve stuffed his lip with a plug of tobacco and slouched next to a short, chubby man in sunglasses and a Mötley Crüe shirt.

"Hey, bra," he said, nodding sagely, his voice a nasally whisper.

"This is Sebastian," Sin D said. "We picked him up in Atlanta. He's got good pills."

"You need anything, bra?"

I stared into his dull eyes. "No thanks."

"Might keep you going all night," Sin D said, pinching my ass.

"No worries, bra, no worries," Sebastian said. He went to the bathroom and left a stench cloud of potato chips, beer, and body odor in his wake.

"Cute," I said.

Jane Doe started laughing. "He's jealous of your new boy-friend, Sin D."

"Fuck your bullshit," Sin D said, and Hardcore Betty gave her a withering look.

They were worn thin from the road and getting grouchier, like they might strangle each other before the show.

Sebastian came back. We unloaded the beer-and-sweat-soaked van, hauled the equipment onstage. Guitar cabinets were missing wheels and the amp heads were missing knobs. The Ampeg bass cabinet was the heaviest thing, big as a coffin, swaths of vinyl peeling off its sides. Jane Doe, for once, actually thanked me.

They made money this time. People bought 45s and t-shirts with *The Porno Sisters* in slashed-up, ransom-letter font over a Pointer Sisters promo picture. While the ladies sold merchandise, Sebastian leaned next to me.

"What's your *thing*, man?" he asked. "What gets you *going*?"

"Writing," I said. "What gets *you* going?"

"Pussy! But you know what I like with my pussy, man? COCAAAAAINE!" To illustrate, he pressed one nostril closed and snorted noisily through the other. Then he air-guitared and hummed the Clapton song for me.

"You're a wild man." I slapped him on the back as hard as I could and went to piss.

When I came back, Sebastian and Sin D were making out. She was biting his beard as he violently gripped her ass. A wave of nausea swept in. I wasn't faithful but expected better. If she saw no difference between me and Sebastian, I might as well be a talking dog's ass.

Hardcore Betty and Jane Doe were holding hands in a booth

while Steve sulked over his guitar, changing strings.

"Let's get the shit and go," I said.

"Better keep the women folk in line, boss man," Sin D said.

Sebastian giggled through his nose.

I cracked open the whiskey at my house and Sin D set Joan Jett spinning on the turntable. All this time spent pining over her and she was wronging me to my face. I dropped ice in a tumbler, poured and sipped. Sin D came in the kitchen smiling.

"You hiding out in here?"

I poured one for her. Jane Doe, Hardcore Betty, and Sebastian were on the back porch, sitting in my wrought-iron chairs. Viciousness rose in me. My body wasn't listening to my mind. *Calm down, calm down.* None of that was getting through.

"So you're fucking your drug dealer."

"Oh shit," she said. "Are you becoming my father?"

"Why? Did you fuck your father too?"

She slapped me so hard I spilled my drink. She tried to bite me. Before I knew it, I had my hand over her mouth. We wrestled and pressed against each other silently for a moment before she broke away and flashed a knife, pulled it from nowhere. I put my arms up.

"YOU GODDAMN MOTHERFUCKER!"

Her eyes were wild with rage. I'd pressed a button without meaning to and was sorry immediately, and scared.

"Put the knife down."

She stood breathing hard and fast, holding the blade between us, spit glistening in the corners of her mouth.

I'd taken some hapkido and thought I could knock the knife out of her hand if I struck both sides of her wrist at once, but I was a little drunk, and likely to slice my own wrists attempting it.

"YOU DON'T KNOW A GODDAMNED FUCKING THING ABOUT ME!"

The glasses on the shelf rang from her voice. I wanted to put my hands over my ears but somehow kept them up in defense. Her eyeliner had run into the pits of her eyes, making her look like a cartoon bandit. But even in her mania, my god, she was beautiful.

"Don't pull a knife on me in my house."

A switch clicked in her brain. "Fine," she said and walked out of the kitchen.

The front door slammed. I was too dumbfounded to move.

Hardcore Betty came in and stared at me. "What did you do?" Then Jane Doe came and both of them left.

She was right: I didn't know much about her. I barely knew myself. I'd once got feedback on a story saying it wasn't clear what motivated my main character. If I wasn't clear about my own motivations, how could I convincingly portray anyone else's? I saw this character, Clay, alone in his kitchen. He never thought he was good enough. Abandoned by his mother. His father chasing the blues. Sin D and Clay didn't have a relationship, only fucking. Now, maybe that was gone.

Sebastian sat on the back porch, enjoying himself. I went out and stood next to his chair.

"Hey, bra," he said, quietly.

"You mind if I sit here?"

He glanced at the other chairs. "No problem, bra."

He got up and sat in the next one. I picked up the chair he'd been sitting in and hurled it out in the yard, where it bounced into the bushes.

I stood next to him again. "You mind if I sit *here?*"

He was slower to answer this time. "Sure bra. Knock yourself out." His voice was, somehow, whinier. He sat in the next chair, very slowly.

I tossed his old one into the yard too. We repeated this exercise until all deck chairs were scattered in the grass.

I stood next to him and stared at the moon, fat as a duck egg. "What do you want out of life, Sebastian? What's your *thing*, bra?"

His eyes were wet. "I want to *live*, man."

I realized I'd cornered him against the railing. I took two steps back and asked for a cigarette. He dug in his denim jacket and lit a Winston for me. We smoked in silence, watching the shadows the trees made on the dewy grass.

"Look man," he whined, "I'm into free love and all that. We're all bros, you know, bra?"

In the moonlight he was almost angelic, some hairy cherub sent from SBG.

"Love is free," I said. "And hate. Hate's free too."

I smoked his cigarettes until he excused himself. I heard the toilet flush, then nothing. After a few minutes I went inside. The front door was wide open with moths slamming against my lamp.

I turned off the spinning record.

REJECTION

The letter on official University of Mississippi stationary said my writing had promise but that I wasn't "quite the right fit for the new program."

It filled me with rage. I didn't need stuffy academics who never worked a factory day in their lives telling me what to do. I didn't need them to write. I'd figure it out on my own. One day they'd wish they'd had me.

I wadded up the paper and ate it just so I could shit it out.

I went through the rest of the day with a stomachache.

OVERTIME

Cabinets Limited started lagging behind. Whoever was ordering wood and supplies kept fucking up which meant everyone on the factory floor had to pay for it with overtime and backbreaking work. The truck would arrive, the driver would back into the loading bay and leave the trailer beckoning, its rear door open, a black hole to fill.

Most of the guys in their forties and fifties wore back braces and wouldn't climb in the truck. That left the youngest but not necessarily the strongest of us to load the trucks. We loaded the heaviest cabinets first. Two men, maybe Big Ollie and Booty Munch, would stand at the back of the trailer and lift the big kitchen cabinets up to us. Me and another young guy, usually somebody destined to quit in two weeks, stacked the cabinets as high as we could. It was hot and stagnant in the trailer. You'd get woozy. Every twenty minutes, I drank from the water cooler while someone took my place.

Management started asking us to stay late. Petty slunk up to me while I slapped cardboard to the cabinets on quality control. "Clay," he said, "think you can stay awhile?" almost bashfully, like asking me to the prom.

"Nope." I stapled a cabinet. "Got plans."

He got this look like he wanted five minutes alone with me in a dark alley. I smiled, showed teeth. He moved along. Somehow, he never fired me, probably because I never said yes even once.

On those overtime days, I clocked out and went home while everybody else called their wives or kids to tell them they'd be late for dinner, don't wait. They might've done something great with those hours away from work.

I figured all I could do was write stories about what they might've done with that time.

THE LORD'S GIFT

In a moldy corner of the coffee shop, I held a chipped mug close to my chest as Audrey sucked her milkshake through a thin straw. She said she needed to tell me something. A painting of some abstract phallus priced at two hundred dollars loomed over our table. The baristas scrambled behind the counter pressing levers.

"I'm over a month late," she said. Her face brightened like it was the greatest news.

I pictured myself holding a baby, its shrill screams, my eyes bloodshot, my hair falling out, my belly grown heavy and round with sorrow. Audrey had won back her body after Caitlin tore through it, but I doubted anyone could come back from that beating twice.

"Are you sure?"

"Of course."

I imagined working some menial job, publishing nothing, a writer failing and floundering like the rest, with a kid in tow.

She put her hand on my knee. "Are you worried?"

"No," I said, "why would I be?" Why would I be worried about the loss of every freedom? "It's just unexpected."

She sat back and studied me. "You know I took precautions." She crossed her legs. "I took the pill at the same time every day." She squeezed my thigh. "Clay," she said, "sometimes the Lord works His mysterious wonders and we have to accept His wisdom. God is trying to tell us something."

"Right," I said. It was my fault. I'd ignored her Southern Baptist God insanity, disregarded her mental state because it had nothing to do with her crotch. But then SBG spread a look of serenity across my face. I didn't have to solve the rest of our lives. I only had to deal with that particular moment and soon, maybe later that night, I could punch myself in the head a few times.

I took her hand and said, "We'll get through this together." I kissed her fingers. I made her laugh.

Then she mentioned maybe we should get married, that Caitlin was beginning to think I was her daddy anyway, and maybe I could move to Tupelo and commute.

I nodded and said reassuring things, taking care never to say yes.

EVERYTHING I OWN IS MADE IN CHINA

I was sweating my ass off at eight in the morning, standing at the router, staring at my Wal-Mart shoes. Everything I owned was made in China. The robotic dremel went back and forth on a rectangle of birch. The same scene I'd watched thirty-five times already.

Life was fucking short and I was going to be a father. All I had until death was my time and how I spent it. This forty-hours-a-week thing was a scam. I figured I could do without a few things. I didn't need the cable TV or that much beer or a subscription to *Penthouse*, for instance. I was burning my life away for the factory owner. Some of these poor hunched bastards, sanding doors all day with dust masks over their noses, had carpal tunnel. Others had withered their brains to gruel. On weekends they medicated with TV, beer, pot, sex, and muscle relaxers. Seeing them was like looking into my future.

I started a story in my head with Sin D as the main character, raging on stages across the country, blowing fire, kicking over the moneychangers' tables. But there was something dark inside keeping her down. She was her own worst enemy. No seed she planted would sprout. She died of an overdose—scratch that. She survived the overdose and stabbed her loser boyfriend in the balls.

Then I imagined an Audrey story. Her hero's heart believed in love and God and liked America the way it already was, like none of it was horseshit. In her story, some asshole knocked her up and abandoned her again. This bent her arc in a new direction. She became a vigilante. She hunted deadbeat dads all over Mississippi, seducing and robbing.

After morning break, I knocked on the office door and told Petty we needed to talk. The AC smelled of stale donuts. I'd memorized what I wanted to say. I knew they wouldn't go for it, I'd need another shitty job.

"I need to work less hours," I said.

He dislodged a chair from under the desk, sat down and lit a cigarette. His eyes lined with tiny branches as he sucked on it.

"You're the best worker we got. We can put you anywhere on the line." He scanned my face. "Something eating at you?"

Lots of things. Becoming a daddy. The indefatigable greed of men. How I was beset, always, by lust. But I narrowed it down. "What's the point in killing myself for this?"

He blew smoke. "How many hours can you work?"

I hadn't anticipated a negotiation. I quickly counted. "Twenty-four. No more than thirty."

"If you can work thirty, we want thirty. We need all the work you can do." We resolved that I'd leave Thursday at one-thirty each week and wouldn't come back until Monday. He nodded. "As long as you work those hours in a row."

Maybe Petty wasn't so bad. We shook hands and I went back to the floor.

By eleven o'clock I was watching the router whine back and

forth on the wood again. The idea that I'd won quickly passed. I was in the same spot, doing the same damn thing.

AUDREY RETURNS TO THE SWIM

She walked in wearing blue scrubs. Must have driven straight from Tupelo for fifty fuming minutes as soon as her shift ended. She hung her purse on the chair and perched on the edge. I sipped my beer cautiously.

"You want a grapefruit juice or ginger ale or something?"

She slammed her fist on the table. People at the bar gawked at us and I stink-eyed them to mind their own business.

"Clay," she said, studying the pint glasses stacked neatly beside the shot glasses. "Why haven't you called me?"

This whole thing between her and SBG had me in knots. "It's just I don't think God had anything to do with it. I mean, people fuck and fuck up. That's how we got pregnant."

She crossed her arms. "God gives us exactly what we need."

"Let's say I'm skeptical."

"Well, I'm not." Her voice jumped a couple volume notches. "I've raised one alone. I can raise two."

The song playing was "Don't Look Back" by Boston. I'd been enjoying it before she came in, but it ended and the room was silent.

"You're right." She pushed the chair back and shouldered her purse. "This isn't about God. It's about your ugly heart."

The beer and whiskey had gone to my legs so I couldn't chase her. Even in scrubs, as she walked out, she looked incredible.

I got drunker and called Mick from quality control when I got home. It rang and rang before he finally answered. I told him it was me. There was static on the line as he sat up grunting. "It's one in the morning, Clay."

"I knocked up a crazy lady."

He chuckled. "Been there myself."

"What did you do?"

"I prayed about it."

"Did that work?"

"My daughter showed up anyway." I heard a Bic flick twice. "But it worked out. Better than I expected."

My hopes sank. The whiskey started sucking me into the mattress.

He had his wife and house in Waterford and drove twenty-five miles to work every day. I told him, sorry, I was just drunk, that I'd drive to him and share a fat joint soon.

I hung up and went to my knees, put my hands together, brought them to my lips.

"My genes are bad," I said. "Life is cruel but I love it even so. I don't know if I can take this, Jesus."

I blacked out and woke up the next morning in wet jeans.

BO DIDDLEY

My last swig of coffee was full of grounds. Somebody knocked as I spat it out in the sink. It was Benton in flannel shirt and work boots.

"Come on in." I had books and magazines and cups everywhere.

He stared at my poster of Johnny Cash giving the finger to Nashville, the framed photograph of Bob Dylan. Stacks of CDs all over the stereo. He pointed to the turntable.

"Needed a new belt," I said. "The old one looked like black chewing gum stretched everywhere." I picked one of the albums I'd taken from him when he'd given up the old Pioneer, Bo Diddley's first.

I cleared some couch space. He sat down listening.

I spent so many hours on the couch with him, my ears trained on the stereo, listening to album after album, while he drank Coors after Coors. When I was a kid, the album covers seemed enormous. All the liner notes, lyrics, and pictures of people who looked like they came from another planet: Sun Ra, Funkadelic, Neil Young, Jimi Hendrix, John McLaughlin, Joni Mitchell, King Crimson. Daddy had hundreds of albums and taught me some chords. I didn't have the patience to practice, but I was still a listener.

He cocked his head to favor his best ear. He had three moles on the back of his neck, purple hull peas that grew darker each year. He never went to the doctor, he just lived permanent as the sky and the trees. We sat listening until "I'm a Man" ended.

"Nobody sounds like that," he said. "You could play the same guitar through the same amp and still not get that sound. Something big is speaking through him."

I considered this.

He slapped me on the knee and asked how I was doing. I told him about Audrey and Caitlin.

"They said you called down at the shop yesterday."

"I wouldn't have, but your phone was off."

He stared across the room, half-embarrassed. "Phone company tried to fuck me over on the bill. I said to hell with it."

"I didn't know how else to get in touch with you."

"Call there anytime," he said. "You're the only one I talk to anyway."

"You want a whiskey drink?" I got up. "I'm going to have one." I went in the kitchen with the glasses, opening the freezer, dropping ice cubes, making noise, trying to ignore the sweat on my nose.

"Water!" he shouted.

I cracked more ice trays, dropped cubes in another tumbler and turned on the tap. I carried the glasses to the living room. He sat on the edge of the couch cushion, his shoulders sloped, hands on his knees. I set the glasses on library books on the coffee table. He picked up his water and read the titles on the spines—*The Hawk Is Dying, Child of God, Cane*—and sipped.

"You read all these?"

"Parts of them."

He took the box of Chesterfields out of his shirt pocket and scanned the room for ashtrays. I snatched a dirty mug from the floor and set it before him. Smoke from his first long drag seeped from his mouth. His whole body seemed to soften.

"It's the first time you've ever called the shop," he said. "Then I come over and you offer me whiskey when you know whiskey makes me mean." He sipped his water. "So where's your head at?"

"I'm going to be a daddy."

"Is that right?"

He flicked ashes in the mug without looking at it. "I guess the apple don't fall far from the tree." He kept fingering some invisible fretboard like he didn't know what to do with his hands if he wasn't knocking dents out of a hood or playing guitar. "You need money?"

"What are you? The Federal Reserve?"

"I'm saying I can help. Mine is yours."

I had student loans I'd probably never pay back. But I pictured him in his trailer on Granddad's land, watching satellite TV every night, holding a beer and cigarette with one hand. Most things were paid for, but he was getting older. He'd be trying to live off Social Security and Army retirement soon.

"We should be good."

He poked my knee with a hard, stubby finger. "You tell me if you need money. Don't be hardheaded."

The needle slipped to the center rings. We sat listening to the rhythmic scratch.

"Well," he said, "flip the damn thing."

THE COWARD

After New Year's, I sold off my shitty furniture, trashed my beer can collection, reduced my life to a dozen cardboard boxes and moved in with Audrey. Another human being was going to see me as God. It scared the hell out of me.

Audrey had never been so happy. We ate vitamins and healthy meals. Her leg hair grew faster and her sex appetite increased, SBG help me. She worked twelve-hour shifts at the hospital and, each night, was tireless in bed. We started tying each other down, whispering nastier things—no need to act out her movies anymore. Whenever Caitlin was away or preoccupied, we gnawed at each other's genitals. In this manner we drugged ourselves. It was a time of deep, endorphined beauty.

I acquired superhuman endurance. I'd get up, write, drive to the factory in Oxford, write, drive to Tupelo, sleep four hours, and do it again. The hair on my arms stood on end. I was always on edge and ready.

One day I needed a break in the pattern, so I called in sick and went to the town square. I ran into Hardy Null, smiling in a short blue dress. Goosebumps up her thighs. High heels, no bra.

"I heard you got your balls sawed off," she said. She had a way with dirty slant rhyme.

"No," I said, pointing, "it's all intact."

"Show me."

Afterwards I told her goodbye. I meant *forever.*

She wiped herself with my boxers and tossed them in the corner. "Try to be good," she said. "I dare you."

My hands shook as I left her apartment. I hadn't eaten all day. I stopped at Ajax Diner and ordered a plate of mashed potatoes, black-eyed peas, macaroni and cheese. I bit into jalapeño cornbread and pretended I wasn't a sorry bastard.

On the drive back to Tupelo, I stared at the hills, cows, horses, trees, and fields. Crows picked dead things off the highway shoulders. This would never work. Pregnant women had heightened powers of perception. Audrey would smell Hardy Null all over, bury her face in my crotch like a hound as soon as I walked in. I decided to charge right in and face the collapse.

Night was coming as I parked in the driveway. It was Audrey's day off and she was in the kitchen and the house smelled of baked chicken, steamed broccoli, peas. Caitlin ran to hug me and went back to her first love, the TV. Audrey hugged me, rubbed my shoulder blades, kissed me. Her brain seemed to receive constant injections of pure joy no matter what.

I talked about the Hemingway, García Márquez, and Flannery O'Connor stories I'd been reading on breaks. She stood at the kitchen counter in old jeans and a t-shirt, hanging on every word.

I told her I needed to write something down before I forgot, something I'd been thinking on the drive, something triggered by the sunset in the rearview mirror.

I went upstairs, got out my journal, and wrote *I'm a sorry bastard. I'm a coward.*

JUMPER ON THE LINE

The old man booked the oyster bar in Tupelo just to visit us. Most of his gigs now were at wannabe juke joints in the Delta where white businessmen were making new money off black music.

The oyster bar filled with folks in jeans and cowboy boots. They bobbed their heads and put down their beers to clap when he finished songs. I sat with Audrey and Caitlin at a picnic table. Caitlin always stayed where we put her and never complained. She watched Benton sweating in the stage lights and told me she liked his gravelly voice. I held Audrey's hand and fingered the white gold engagement ring I'd given her.

He plucked and scratched his way through "Jumper on the Line." His voice, hoarse from decades of cigarettes, hit the higher notes in a raspy whisper. He didn't have the right voice or skin color, but he got the song across, the longing and hurt.

The bar owner had agreed to pay him a percentage of drink sales, which wasn't much, but it covered expenses. He'd had to replace some of the tubes in his amp, and they weren't cheap. I stood at the foot of the stage as he packed up.

He slapped the top of his Fender Vibrolux amp. "I don't like how this damn thing sounds now. Too chimey."

When I was Caitlin's age he'd smash beer bottles if the sound wasn't right. He once punched a drunk soundman.

"Sounded great out front," I said.

Caitlin appeared at my side. "Grandpa," she said. She'd only met him once before.

"There's my girl." He put down the cable he was rolling up and knelt down to hug her. "There she is."

"Will you play for us later?" Caitlin said. "Will you play for my birthday party?"

"Don't give him a big head," I said.

He laughed. "Maybe. But I only play for good girls. Are you a good girl?"

She said she was.

Daddy played a quiet, sweet "This Land Is Your Land" to put Caitlin to bed. We sat at the kitchen table and pushed empty Budweisers toward the middle as we finished them. Audrey had an early shift and went to bed. I fixed the couch, tucked a sheet over the cushions, spread blankets, put out two pillows. I followed him out on the porch for his last cigarette of the night.

It was cold, no light from the new moon. He coughed and retched while I pretended it wasn't going on as long as it was.

"Cute little girl she's got," he said, catching his breath and pointing upstairs. "Just the sweetest thing." He tossed the cigarette out in the grass and jammed his fists in his pockets. "If this works, it might be good for you. I thought you didn't need this at first. But it can work if you want it to."

When I was a kid I always felt he could read my mind a little. I didn't know exactly how much I took after him with women and drinking, but I had my suspicions.

"I want it to work," I said, "but sometimes it feels like I'm sabotaging it. Like I can't accept the good life." I knocked on the wood of the back door. "I get restless."

He stood closer to me. "You don't want the other life. It's nothing special."

"You do all right."

"You're not as tough as me. You grew up drinking all the co-colas you wanted."

"They rotted my teeth."

"You never went without is what I'm saying. I didn't have anything growing up." He shifted his weight, favoring one leg over the other. "If you grow up seeing the people you love knocking each other around, you think that's the way it should be. That's love. But it's not true."

I put my hand on his shoulder. "I'm sure Mom forgave you."

No tears in his eyes when he looked at me. Just weight.

"Let's go back in," I said.

We tried not to wake Audrey and Caitlin. I convinced him to lie down.

Next morning the sun rode low and yellow, barely over the trees. I wandered downstairs in my underwear. The blankets and sheets were folded and stacked on the middle couch cushion with the pillows leaned against them.

TAR PIT

When I told Audrey how much I loved writing, sometimes she'd get excited with me. Other times she'd just stare at the television. One time she started talking about church.

"You really should come with me and Caitlin. I told the pastor about you."

I didn't want to step into this tar pit, but I had no choice. "Me and God have an understanding where we don't go to each other's houses."

"It's the way we do things," Audrey said, pulling her bangs.

"It's the way *you* do things, baby."

She showed me the sad face, the breaker of men. "It's what families do together."

I bit my lips and tried not to get angry. How many times did I have to repeat myself? "Families live different ways," I said. "Don't the three of us have a great time?"

"Yes," she said, holding her stomach. "I just worry about you."

"I worry about all of us. Heaven I don't worry about. I worry about *this* world."

We sat with the TV noise.

"Clay, I read one of your stories in your journal." She started crying. "I know you told me not to," she sobbed, "but why don't you write about nice things?"

I put my arm around her. I told her, again, nothing was finished, that I didn't like happy endings, and that she didn't understand the process.

"Is our life really that horrible?" She leaned against me and cried.

And I was so angry as I held her.

DEAD MOTHERFUCKERS OF LITERATURE

I became an insomniac, sneaking out of Audrey's house to sit in my truck. The other houses stood on all sides, crammed on third-of-an-acre lots. Closed garage doors and home security signs. Nobody had enough yard, windows, light, or trees. It was a farm where the houses were crops and we were insects eating away at the insides.

Stories came to me. People with dark secrets and closed hearts trying to make life beautiful together. Something always ripped it apart. The characters destroyed themselves and those they loved. Houses and new cars and children to raise to be better than them, but it never worked out as planned. Despite their intentions, they were terrible to each other.

I wrote in a journal I kept under the driver's seat of my truck. Sipped out of a pint of Kentucky Tavern stashed in the glove compartment and wrote until I couldn't keep my eyes open, the moon skipping like a stone across the sky. Then I crept back in the house, just falling asleep when Audrey's alarm went off.

She went in at seven, got off at seven. I started writing again
as soon as I heard the garage door close. During her weekend
shifts, I went to the bookstore in Oxford and communed with the
dead motherfuckers of literature. I lost myself, let the words enter
my bloodstream with the caffeine. Sometimes there was another
writing bout in the late afternoon, sometimes not. I'd hit happy
hour and, by the time she got off work, be in Tupelo for dinner.

Her belly grew like she'd swallowed a globe. I provided foot
rubs, hand rubs, head rubs, hand jobs. Her body bloomed by my
touch. But after she fell asleep, I lay thinking about the journal
under the truck seat and the pint, the people in the houses. Soon
enough, like in a dream of falling, I'd be there.

LOVE

I was sitting at The Swim minding my own business.

I'd taken Audrey to the Justice of the Peace the day before. We
got married in a side room with plastic flowers stapled to the wall.
The judge stood behind a podium and said words too vague to
describe what marriage actually meant—the end of freedom and,
possibly, animal pleasure. This was my sacrifice to the child coming
into this world.

Hardy Null walked through the door in a low-cut dress.

"You mind?" she said, sitting down.

"I'm just drinking."

"You look a little different," she said, tossing her cigarette pack
on the bar. "Are you in love?"

"I'm always in love."

She crossed her legs, made a production of it. "I know what
you love." The bartender brought her a Budweiser.

"What's that?"

                                                          Max Hipp

"Yourself." She flashed hard eyes at me. "If you could fuck yourself, you'd never leave the house."

In the bar mirror, I studied the face I'd gazed into, the body I'd writhed against. How many hours had I spent with this woman who thought such things of me? Audrey didn't think that. She worshipped me.

"Don't take it so hard," she said. "It takes one to know one."

I killed my beer and got up.

"Aw. Why don't you sit and be nice?" She smiled and propped her slender, sun-browned arms on the bar.

I said, "You're not the only woman in town."

"Tell her hello."

Outside, the loneliness was lurking. It stood in the tops of the trees, whipped the flags around, flowed in my lungs and rattled in my ribcage.

DEAD INSIDE

I kept thinking of lines from The Porno Sisters song, "Dead Inside."

> *There's nowhere to run,*
> *nowhere to hide*
> *when you're dead inside*
> *you're dead inside*

And the bridge:

> *You stare at the abyss*
> *and the abyss stares back.*

Over and over.

BOOTY MAN

I was spending a lot of daylight ripping down pine boards with the panel saw. I stood at the machine all morning and watched it clamp and cut. Even though I was inhaling chemicals, I loved the scent of pine hot from the saw.

During the afternoon break, Booty Munch sat in the office talking up Becky, who issued the payroll checks. She'd given me shit one day for waiting to cash my check.

She said, eyeing me suspiciously, "Everybody else cashes theirs right away, and you wait until the next Wednesday."

I just smiled and nodded. It was none of her damn business.

I clocked out that day and Becky got in the car with Booty.

He got in and rolled down the tinted windows halfway. He nodded at me, proud, like, *You seeing this?* "Later, College Boy," he said.

SIDNEY ARNOLD MEEKS

He popped out covered in gore, pissing on the doctor. I'd never been prouder of any creature nor so overcome with ecstatic love. I wanted to plaster his tiny purple face on the billboards up and down I-55.

Upstairs, in his room, I held him. Sidney Arnold Meeks. Sid. S.A.M. I stood by the window while he slept in my arms. Audrey was in the kitchen, grinding ice for margaritas, happy to finally drink again. My father and mother had held me this way—how strange and wonderous it must've felt. Warm, heavenly flesh and new cries in the night.

I admired the mimosa hanging over the yard. Sun lit up the west in pinks and oranges. The clouds hung high and wide. It was too much beauty. I wept.

Audrey called me down for drinks, but I couldn't put him back in his crib, couldn't take us from the window, the view, the light.

THANKSGIVING

Thanksgiving rolled around and everyone was supposed to leave at noon. After the ten o'clock break Petty shuffled up to quality control.

"We need to work overtime," he said. He started to go tell somebody else the same thing.

"It's a half-day," Mick said. "Goddamn Thanksgiving."

Petty turned around, his face smooth as a bullet. "We work overtime today, Mick." He walked away, his back hunched a bit at the top of his spine.

Mick's hands shook as he drilled the screws, his mouth tightened to a slit. I figured he'd fling a cabinet across the factory floor any minute.

"You staying for this shit?"

It didn't matter what I did or what they did to me. I was a tourist. A writer destined for bigger things despite what the MFA fuckers had said.

"Naw," I said, "fuck that."

I shouldn't have said it that way, with him wound up. The job was his livelihood.

"Damn right." He spat in the dust. "I'm getting the fuck out of here. I'm going home to eat turkey with my wife."

When the lunch buzzer rang I clocked out and walked through the loading bay doors as quickly as possible. Mick followed close behind. I felt the eyes on us and met him at my tailgate.

"Well," he smiled, "you have a good Thanksgiving."

"You too." We shook hands.

The following Monday Mick wasn't at quality control, the only place he ever worked.

"Fired," Petty said.

As he went back toward the office, I started to wish him a heart attack but quickly took it back. Petty's existence was punishment enough.

The router cut its grooves. I pretended nobody had any power over me, nothing could get me down.

I imagined a story where the foreman of a factory got stuck in the machines he claimed to control. The routers bit his flesh. They etched deep chambers into his skin.

DEPARTURE

I thought, despite my general fuckups, that things with Audrey were going well, even better than expected.

One night I came home to her crying on the couch. I asked what was wrong. She retreated to the kitchen. When I followed, she went upstairs, and I climbed after her.

Her packed suitcases stood on wheels just inside the bedroom door.

"I'm taking Sid and Caitlin and we're going tomorrow."

I'd stopped cheating because it was wrong, but maybe she'd found out anyway. She looked so good heartbroken, I wanted her more than anything.

I asked why she wanted to leave.

She sighed. "God's not in your heart like He's in mine. He doesn't live in you." She stared, into me. "I don't see how you can be in these times without God." There was such pain in her face, her lips tightened around each word. "How do you do it, Clay?"

It was about the baptism. She wanted Sid baptized, and I

didn't, which was more than she could take. It was destroying her.
I wanted to tell her that she was confusing God and church. Then
tell her all the reasons why there was no God, proving some worn-
out point that wouldn't help.

"I just carry on," I said. "As far as I can tell, that's all anybody
does."

That night I made love to her, saying goodbye to us. Afterward,
I didn't sleep. I tried not to move, wanted to feel her warmth before
it slipped away.

I helped her with the bags the next morning, arranged them in
her car the best that I could. She was going to her mother's until I
could find another place.

I kissed Caitlin on both cheeks. I strapped Sid into the car seat
and kissed his bald head. He dropped his pacifier and stared at me,
a world cooling and hardening behind his deep blue eyes.

All I could do was wave as my family backed out of the driveway.

SUSHI

I moved back to Oxford, found a house near the center of town. I
convinced a jogger to help me move a couch somebody had set out
for trash to the back porch, where I steam vacuumed and sprayed it
with Febreze and left it drying in the sun.

The first thing I set up was the record player, the receiver and
the speakers. I dropped the needle on Skynyrd's "On the Hunt"
and "Simple Man" to raise the hairs on my arms. Ronnie Van Zant
sang me strong again.

Days in fat city with Audrey were over. Child support was
going to have to come from somewhere and the factory job alone
wouldn't cut it, so I got a side gig on the weekend at Two Stick
where I'd met Sin D. There'd been enough turnover that the

remaining waitresses were fuzzy on the details about exactly why they hated me. I smiled and flirted. Soon we were getting along again, like one big two-faced family.

I pressed the rice to the paper, shaped it with the bamboo mat, cut sushi into pieces and arranged it on the plate as good as anybody. I sweated under the lights, trying not to slice my fingers off.

Another factory, every bit as dangerous and twice as nerve-wracking.

SUNDAY NIGHT FOOTBALL

Daddy's friend across the highway had bush-hogged. Grass lay scooped in piles along the driveway. I pulled in and set his mailbox back on its post. He'd rigged it once already with chicken wire that I used to wrap and fasten it again.

He was spending most of his afternoons on the deck behind his trailer. I sat in the folding chair beside him. He handed me a beer from the cooler. We watched the tall trees sway and buzzards circle above them, high and sun-drenched on the wind.

"How're my grandbabies?"

"Growing like weeds." I took the photos out of my wallet. Caitlin showing her front teeth in her school picture. Sid in a blue jumper. Each day it sank me, how much I was missing. It made me finish my beer and start another.

"Man," Benton said, "the ladies are gonna love Sid."

We finished more beers as the sun went down. He went inside and put potatoes in the oven. I poured charcoal in his rusty grill and doused it with lighter fluid. It lit with a *whoosh*.

We ate well done burgers. I told him I didn't know how I was going to pay child support for the rest of my life. He just shook his head.

"That's the price of letting a good woman go."

I put my fork down. "I did everything in my power to make her happy. And she left *me*."

"You're kidding yourself," he said, chewing the meat.

"What do you know about it?"

"Son," he said, "Audrey might not have caught you running around but that don't mean you didn't do it."

"I didn't," I said, but I could feel myself grinning, sorry bastard that I am.

"It's in your nature. But that don't make it okay. She could feel it even if she didn't see it. They always do."

I told him he was wrong, that she'd decided I wasn't holy enough for her. He just grunted and said, "Is that all it is?"

After dinner, I sat in the recliner, watching TV, trying to drink up the strength to drive home. In the morning I woke on his couch. The buzzards were up again, circling like kites from hell.

NEW RECORD

The Porno Sisters were putting out a new LP and playing the Caledonia Lounge in Athens. Stieglitz, the new guy, owed me and covered my weekend sushi shifts. I packed a bag on Friday morning and pointed the truck east.

I sat on a shaky stool and stared at the prices taped to the beer bottles, the Christmas lights encircling them. The Porno Sisters had already loaded in and set up, probably getting high in the green room. I was one of the first, but people steadily trickled in. I drank whiskey sours until my throat felt coated with high-fructose corn syrup. Garage rock blasted through the house PA and the room came alive with drunken cackling.

Sin D, hair frizzed and streaked pink, crashed through the

exit door and set a bucket of beers onstage. She wore black jeans and a new Motörhead t-shirt with sleeves and collar cut off, her arms cordy and veined. Stiff Steve, Hardcore Betty, and Jane Doe hopped onstage. There was feedback, a few snare and kick hits, shrill guitar noise, and off they went.

It was the best I'd seen them. They fed off of the hometown friends, snapped up the energy and shot it back. Steve swayed like a robot nailed to the stage. Sin D had some new moves. She held the cable and swung the microphone out over the crowd before drawing it in and singing at the last moment. She kept pulling High Lifes from their five-gallon paint bucket, shaking them and spraying the audience. People started sliding. In the middle of the crowd, I forgot the money troubles and the hell of my loneliness. It was enough to exist with the joy of warm blood in your veins. Rock and roll blasted the air, built to die, like all of us.

After the show, Sin D stood in a crowd by the stage. Her mascara ran and her sweat-soaked shirt clung to her body. She talked with lots of nodding and laughing, touches of deafness, joy, and shellshock. I held the LP under my arm and waited for her to see me, but she never did. I walked over. She nodded and listened to a man in a Porno Sisters shirt talk about some obscure show from three years ago. She gave him a hug and he wandered off.

She glared at me. "The fuck are you doing here?"

I put my hands up. "I'm unarmed. I came to see the show and buy a record." I leaned and took a Sharpie from the table. "Will you sign this?"

The album was called *I'm So XXXcited*. The cover was a black-and-white picture of a Russ Meyer girl's torso with a goat head for a face. She snatched the album and the marker and scrawled FUCK U across it.

"Beautiful," I said. "Where's the afterparty?"

She put her hands on her hips. A tiny shard of hatred melted from her eyes. "You can ride with us. You can't stay with me."

"I just wanted to see the show," I said. "I don't want the night to end yet. That's all."

"Cool," she said. "Help us load out."

Jane Doe and Hardcore Betty wouldn't speak to me even when I helped them move the coffin bass cabinet. We crammed everything into the van, which now stank of dog shit. Sin D sat in my lap as we rode to the party. Ten minutes later, we reached a house at the end of a cul-de-sac, cars parked in the yard and against every curb.

Someone had shot out most of the streetlights. The brightest stars and planets were nailed above Athens. As I watched everyone walk toward the house, I had a twinge of hopelessness. What the hell was I doing? Why did it matter? It mattered because of Sid and Audrey and Caitlin. Their bright names fastened to the sky. Without them, I was dark. I pulled out my notepad and attempted to jot down what the night felt like. I could write my way through darkness, maybe even redeem myself with words.

Then the whiskey hit me harder and I stopped thinking altogether.

Kegs of beer, joints passed around. The people who lived in the dilapidated mansion were passed out in recliners and across the fireplace with *cockmonger* scrawled on their foreheads, giving the party the feel of a mutiny. The living room was completely dark and filled with people from the show geeking out on Dead Boys, Gun Club, The Sonics.

Sin D was surrounded by boys with rocker haircuts. I went to the kitchen keg, pumped two cups of beer, and squeezed through the crowd next to her.

"It's not much of a party unless you dance with me," she said.

We shimmied and jumped and howled. I wanted her to need me more than anything, to feel like she'd self-destruct without me. She pressed her body against mine. I didn't care anymore how many other guys were in her orbit. My wife had stopped loving me but not Sin D. She was crazy enough to keep at it.

After a few rounds of sweating I followed her up the grand staircase. Dead things hung in the cobwebs in the high corners. Drunks leaned against the railing. I pushed her into the first bedroom and shut the door.

Thousands of comic books in plastic sleeves, no doubt worth something in the idiot future, were stacked around a mattress with a soiled navy-blue sheet lumped on top. The floorboards were ashy, and in the corner stood a dusty, upright piano lined with squeezed beer cans.

"Nice places you take me," she said.

I stared at her with a raw burning. Her pupils were big as dimes, dark as motor oil.

She slapped my face. It didn't hurt.

"You think I was just waiting for you?" She grabbed my beltloops and pulled me toward her. "Motherfucker, I'll eat you like air."

USELESS

On factory days, I got up at five, ran around the block, and went home to start writing before work. I tried to finish a story in one sitting. If I couldn't flesh the whole thing out, I'd have the skeleton at least and could fill in the rest later. I wrote with a clear mind, like taking dictation. A few good lines here and there, little sprinklings of truth—that's all I needed. But I didn't finish anything.

It didn't take Audrey long to start seeing a guy who worked

at a bank. This hit so deep, I couldn't even feel it. She got good at reminding me what a sonofabitch I was too.

"You've got kids. Remember?" she said on the phone, like I wasn't working two jobs.

"You got my check, right?"

"This isn't about any check. It's about seeing your babies, Clay."

Since she was screwing this finance guy, I was just another child to deal with. Self-centered, stubborn, and useless, maybe I *was* a child. I decided to push her buttons.

"I went to church the other day," I lied.

"You're kidding."

"Sat through a sermon about forgiveness of sins."

Her voice softened. "What did you think?"

I told her it was fine. She suggested I go every Sunday. I could even drive to Tupelo and go to church with her, Caitlin, Sid, and the financier. I could drool next to her like a degenerate, black-sheep stepson.

I got angry thinking about that scene but managed to keep it inside long enough to hang up.

AUDREY AT TWO STICK

One sushi-rolling night, Audrey came in wearing a skirt and stared me down. She and the banker followed the hostess to a table. She climbed the stool and crossed her legs in the candlelight. He wore a dress shirt tucked into khakis, belly bulging over the belt. He'd combed a few hairs over his bald hump.

I made the tickets, humiliated. He had his hand on her elbow, ogling her over his glasses like the kind of guy who dates his secretaries. Audrey was giving his secretaries a run for their money while my hands were in fish, shrimp, eel, crab, and seaweed. She brought him in just to make it clear she didn't belong to me, no one belonged to anybody.

The way I saw it, she gave me no choice. She wanted it this way. But I'd ruined my best thing and maybe deserved to lose another family.

About this time, I sliced an avocado and cut through the edge of my thumb. I went in back before I bled all over the rice. The waitresses, cooks, managers, dishwashers, and bartenders streamed past me while I rummaged in the first aid kit for a bandage. I cut off the thumb of a rubber glove. I washed the cut until the bleeding slowed, and then put on the bandage and topped it with the rubber thumb.

By the time I got back to the stacked-up tickets, Audrey and the banker were gone. They hadn't been able to keep their hands off each other long enough to eat.

BENTON MEEKS

I'd just lay down after a night of Irish Car Bombs when the sheriff's department called saying he was sorry but Benton Meeks was dead. He'd been coming from Clarksdale on Highway 6 and crossed the median into a trailer transporting a mobile home. The kid had tried to dodge him and was pretty broken up about it. But in my head, he was playing "Will the Circle Be Unbroken" and "I Saw the Light."

I sobered up fast, angry like there was someone to blame. Of the millions of bastards to pluck from this world—why him? I felt cheated and more alone than ever.

I don't remember getting into the car. At the hospital, I hovered between the fluorescent lights and waxed floors. I heard the *squeak* of my shoes but couldn't feel my legs. It didn't occur to me to call anyone, that anyone could help.

                                                                    Max Hipp

I met a deputy and went down to the morgue. It was like the rest of the hospital except it smelled even stronger of disinfectant. We found the wall of drawers. This man grabbed the handle on the huge filing cabinet, put his weight into it until the drawer glided out. A pear-shaped body under the sheet. I closed my eyes for a second or two and held my breath.

"Are you okay with this?"

I looked at the man speaking, his mustache and thick hair. I told him I could handle it. The sheet came back. Daddy was bruised and swollen in the face.

"It's him," I said.

I signed the death certificate and listened to the deputy again. The car was demolished along with his Fender Vibrolux and the '52 Fender Telecaster. Later, they gave me a plastic bag with his wallet and steel slide. They said it looked like a stroke, like he died before impact.

"In any case, he didn't suffer."

The arrogance of motherfuckers talking about his suffering. You could hear the hurt when he played and sang.

His body was on the slab, but Daddy had escaped.

I couldn't gather any emotion into my voice when I called Audrey. Just told her and listened to her break down. Her heart was always tender for him.

There were things he never got to say to my mother before she died. I regretted that for him, and I regretted the things I'd never get to tell Benton. I couldn't remember the last time I told him I loved him.

A little before dawn I drove to St. Peter's Cemetery, down the narrow roads between the graves, and parked next to the shed where they housed the mowers. I needed to see Daddy's resting place before he got there. I walked to the crest of the hill overlooking a valley of headstones, sat on a grave under a cedar and watched the sky lose the night.

ONE MORE SONG

My legs were skinny in the black suit pants. I had to tighten the belt an extra notch. I stood at the entrance to the funeral parlor and greeted people, some I didn't know, and old family friends and distant relatives whose names I couldn't remember. They hugged me and clapped me on the back. *Clap clap clap* on my baggy coat.

Audrey came with my mother-in-law and Sid and Caitlin. I took Sid out of the stroller and hugged him while he sucked on his pacifier. I put him back and my mother-in-law took the kids into the chapel.

Audrey looked lovely in her black dress. I wanted to hold her in front of the family and the funeral director and everybody and tell her how much I needed her. She stood to the side and helped me greet everyone lining up. It was good to see people acting decently.

After a while, the funeral director said he was going to usher everyone into the sanctuary, that it was best for the family to go first so everyone could take the cue. Audrey and the kids sat up front with me. The sanctuary was set up like a fake church. My stiff collar itched my neck. But I looked at the kids and took it. Caitlin was crying. I told her Benton was in heaven now, playing guitar, he'd be with us forever in the songs. When I pulled Daddy's slide from my pocket, she held it with both hands like it might fly away.

People shuffled in, clunked against the pews. Canned organ music bleated through tiny speakers hidden in the rafters. Men in suits talking about old times wasn't Benton's world. He'd grown up with it, but church made him uneasy.

He'd left only one instruction about how he wanted to be buried.

                                                Max Hipp

Many times, he'd told me, "Play something good at my grave." At first I didn't have any ideas. He liked Fred McDowell, Son House, Skip James, R. L. Burnside. He played their songs, loved the way they choked and bent the strings. I remembered an untitled song he played on an album recorded in Como, a song full of jangle and howl.

We rode to the cemetery under a ceiling of low gray clouds and walked to the forest-green tent about forty yards from Faulkner's grave. I set the boombox on the Astroturf beside the casket. His guitar and voice rang out. It was just a song, but his magic was there. I remembered the ashtrays of my youth as it played, time spent in trailers and bars, long drives in his truck. Nothing stitched us together but songs the dead passed down.

When the song was done we lowered Benton Meeks down.

We went back to the car, everyone trying to walk on wet grass in dress shoes and high heels. I put my lips against Sid's fuzzy ear and strapped him into the car seat. Audrey kissed my cheek, said to call if I needed anything. We said goodbye.

Nobody'd be at my funeral because I'd drive them all away. I'd die alone, cold, and broke. And darkness would cover my eyes and the name would be erased, and woe is me—cue the violins.

Still, I was grateful to know him for a while.

LEFTOVERS

I did the payment plan with the funeral home. He left me the trailer and the land. I didn't see how I could keep it.

There didn't seem to be any real families anymore, only people who kept some superficial contact for the duration of their lives. Maybe I was agnostic about family. My ancestors had worked their asses off, generation after generation dropping dead in the dirt year after year, toiling for a faster, smarter, more ruthless man's profit.

What did it matter?

I didn't care about any of them but the old man. He'd done something. He'd *lived*.

The trailer smelled like WD-40 and French fries. His bed was dented in the middle. For a week after he died, I went to town only for liquor and frozen dinners. I'd wake in the morning, vomit, and finish off what was left, some hair of the dog for the maggots in my brain.

He had hundreds of channels. I'd sit transfixed by bullshit, brainwashed by ads and half-assed Hollywood stars. The TV shows seemed broadcast from another planet. The easy dramas, laughs, and boobs sucked me right in.

I missed all my factory shifts and drove out in the county, looked at bean fields, creeks, cows, goats, horses, and, mostly, the sky. I was angry at words and wrote nothing but a haiku:

Cows kneel in pastures
Lightning ricochets cloud to cloud
But no rain to fall

I sat and waited for the twilight frogs to call from the ditches as headlights washed over me, passing cars accelerated and moved on. Lights came on in distant windows. Cool air settled and spread across the Yocona River bottom.

I wrote at Benton's kitchen table. It was covered with broken strings, broken tubes, and pieces of guitar cables he'd tried to fix. I slipped his slide on my finger and tapped the window.

Night swelled with stars out on his deck and I was left with a dull heaviness, like I'd swallowed hurt, maybe death herself. Owls perched in the trees, loneliness freighting the air.

　　　　　　　　　　　　　　　　　　　　　　　Max Hipp

Hunger pains hit and subsided.

POSTCARD II

One crap day I checked my mail in town and found an envelope addressed in shaky blue ink, no return address. Inside was a single Polaroid picture of an enormous uncircumcised erection.

There was a hand giving the thumbs up sign in the upper right corner, black nail polish and bullet bracelet a la Sin D Porno. Written in the white space below the picture were the words *Found: Divine Hammer*.

I burned the motherfucker on my grill. Watched it twist like a tortured flower.

There are some bigger but I don't need proof.

LAST DAY

I went back to the factory to get my check, expecting to get cussed and canned. I walked in the loading dock door with no saws screaming. The air was clear of dust.

Petty waved me into the office, told me he was sorry about my dad.

I asked what happened.

"We're finished," he said.

Turned out Booty Munch and Becky had run some kind of embezzling racket. She was watching the account, snatching money here and there, not enough for the owner, Bill, to notice. She started giving Booty Munch thirty dollars an hour. It had gone on for six months or so, but they'd fucked up. Victoria's Secret charges had appeared on the expense account.

"Bill had enough. He's got the business up for sale."

Big Ollie and everybody in the spray room and on the assembly line. What would they do? The whole world had capsized.

"This is awful, Petty."

"You said it."

I went out into the parking lot with my last check, half-employed and full depressed.

THE SEA

I drank alone at the house, solemnly and efficiently, like it was my job. I rolled sushi for assholes. I wallowed in self-pity. If I couldn't write, at least I could live the writer's life, burning out furiously, like a fuse to nothing.

I talked to Audrey on the phone. I couldn't stop talking after I'd had a few. I told her it was shitty when bad things happened to good people, but no matter what you did, bad things were going to happen. She agreed the few times I was right. When I was wrong, she just listened.

The financier was out of the picture. On one of his international expeditions he'd found some Brazilian dancer. No matter what Audrey talked about—her wheezing car, the politics at the hospital, her aching feet, the mortgage—it sounded comforting. I imagined her, Caitlin, and Sid up in the house. I dreamed about going on vacation sometime in the future, Sid's eyes lighting up at his first sight of the sea, his fear of the waves, and then: joyful surrender to the water, this force stronger than him, the unknown.

GLORY

The air felt like bathwater the day Audrey showed up with Sid. Her dress clung to the light sweat on her thighs. They looked like a Madonna and child out of some Renaissance painting out on the porch, come to see an alcoholic redneck.

She surveyed the beer cans on every surface, the fast food bags and cups. I cleared clothes off the couch. I held Sid. He smelled like a heaven of warmth and goodness and soggy diapers.

"Clay," Audrey said, "Sid and Caitlin need a daddy."

She looked hot and maternal, like at the ice cream shop the day we'd met. I told her I'd go to church, the moon, anywhere for her.

Maudlin fuck that I am, I teared up.

A LATE ENCOUNTER

I couldn't write anything but tiny two-hundred-word stories. The dead stopped speaking through me. The wind in my mind died. I hoped someday I'd come back to these stories and stitch them into something coherent but wasn't holding my breath.

It was Sunday, and Audrey was working. I dropped Sid and Caitlin with Audrey's mother and ran errands I'd been putting off. I charged a hundred dollars' worth at the supermarket and filled Audrey's trunk with bags of groceries. I bought a new stopper, one with a better seal, to stop the toilet from running. It felt good to complete small tasks. I could focus on what was in front of me, on things I could do something about.

I pulled into a gas station and got out to fill the tank.

A shiny red Toyota pulled up to the pump in front of me. Long legs spilled out and there stood Hardy Null. She grabbed the pump and stuck it in her car and pulled the trigger, the hem of her dress brushing gently against her thighs, her legs browned and inviting.

My line jumped and quit and she still hadn't seen me. I could've driven off. But I set the nozzle back in the cradle and walked over.

She studied me from head to toe.

"Where's the kid, Daddy?"

"Mother-in-law's. What you doing in town?"

Our entire orgasmic history seemed to flash across her face.

"Looking for you."

There was a motel across the street. Thirty-nine ninety-nine. The groceries would be fine. It wouldn't take long enough for anything to spoil.

I followed her car and considered the strangeness of life, how it was worth it despite the cost, even the moments of howling ugliness.

The rusty staircase rang hollowly as we climbed. A maid pushed her cart along the walk and looked away, uninterested. People lied to themselves so they could go on killing themselves every day. My characters did the same.

The key card swiped through the slot and the door opened. Hardy walked into the dark room, pulled the dress over her head, threw it on the television. She sat down, no underwear, and stared at me.

I stood in the doorway and closed my eyes, listened to the traffic swell and deflate through the intersections. In the distance the highway thrummed with people driving home. Kids shouted out of school bus windows.

"Well," she said, "I don't have all day."

I didn't open my eyes. There was nothing to see—I knew what came next.

But I imagined a story where the main character went to that gas station and saw the woman parked at the pump. She didn't see him, and he let her go by. He was better off without her. A better man now than he used to be, a stronger one. He didn't go to any motel. He put the gas pump back in the cradle and drove the groceries home to his family.

LAST YEAR'S MAN

He came in wearing a porkpie hat, the ripped top painted like a ladybug. Melted-looking rubber nose, greasepaint five o'clock shadow. He carried a blanket tied to a stick.

I pushed aside my empty and the bartender brought another. The clown sat next to me and pretended to fish for my beer, casting and reeling until the bartender slid him one. He downed half of it, then frowned, moved his fist under his eye, poked out his bottom lip. One eye hung lower, like that side of his face was older than the other.

Sheila and Abigail were waiting for me at home. In counseling, I'd discovered I'd been squashing down my feelings. I wasn't sure which ones to hold and which to let go. Sometimes tending to the bad ones felt like swinging at ghosts in the dark. I was making progress, sure, but a hole had opened in me. What do you put in the hole?

The clown's pants were made of patches. He slipped a tiny pair exactly like them on his fingers and walked them across the bar. He stood and pointed to me, then his plaid tie, then the door.

"That's two-fifty," the bartender said.

The clown started turning his pocket inside-out. The insides went on forever, piling at his feet.

"I got it," I said.

He re-stuffed his pocket, picked up his blanket-on-a-stick. When he got to the door he turned around and cast his imaginary fishing line, his low eye wide as he tried to reel me in.

A river of taillights shined ahead. Traffic backed up for a few exits and came to a standstill. What got me through the commute and the paralegals scrambling to hold the door, the pitiful glances in the elevator, was Sheila's chicken piccata and salad. She showed love through food and fussing over Abby and me.

I propped my phone against the wheel to watch Abby bang tiny fists on the yellow high chair, her mouth grape-juice purple. When the video cut off, there was a distant siren and honking, and flashing red lights in the rearview. The headlights of cars behind me cleared a path, a chaos of parting metal as the fire truck closed in.

The hole inside me yawned wide.

I pulled to the shoulder, my guts knotting in my throat as the red monster roared through, the siren pitch-shifting before fading away. I cried.

The house would be dark again, the fridge stuffed with takeout bags. I knew what twenty tons of firetruck did to flesh and why families shouldn't have open coffins.

I used to wonder how humans could hold truth and fabrication in the mind simultaneously, even switching between the two, believing what someone else would never stomach. I didn't wonder anymore.

I could taste the dill on the chicken and the salad's vinaigrette. Smoky wine the color of roses.

Down the interstate, I passed a man in the shadows. His silhouette in my mirrors, I could just make out the stick slanting over his shoulder with a teardrop-shaped bundle at the end.

                                        Max Hipp

The firm said I needed time off. A leave of absence.

My first Monday home, I ditched my counseling appointment and looked up what the clown had been carrying. It was called a *bindle*.

That afternoon, I drove to fire station no. 3 looking for Flubber. Like some cruel joke, the man who'd demolished my life was named Fred Flubber. His picture had been in the paper. He was prematurely balding and wore wire-rimmed glasses.

I'd driven to the station before, but this time I got out. Within a minute, he appeared from the garage wearing yellow coveralls and a black shirt, waving like he'd been waiting for me.

"Mr. Pendleton," he said. "I'm sorry I didn't reach out." He had the build of a lumberjack with the face of an accountant. "I'm so sorry, Mr. Pendleton, it's just the worst thing."

I clenched my fists at chest level as this man, a foot taller than me, broke down.

Flubber went on living in the world he'd rid of Sheila and Abby. Due to incompetence. Due to plowing through an intersection to get to a fire in an abandoned building. Due to Sheila not seeing or hearing him coming. Due to so many coincidences the mind couldn't parse them and pain had no beginning or end.

"Let me take off my glasses before you hit me." He knelt on the asphalt and removed them one ear at a time. In his clear, moist eyes I saw someone else to pity.

Behind him, flower boxes bloomed below the firehouse windows. Two butterflies flitted on the marigolds.

In dreams, Sheila's dry palm in mine, we went to the supermarket. Abby's legs dangled from the cart and she said *flutterby* and *Daddy silly*, the sweetest sounds I ever heard. Waxed aisles stretched ahead luxuriously as we dropped dream items in the basket.

I daydreamed about them too, whole afternoons spent staring at vines choking the azaleas in Sheila's flowerbed, imagining the places we could've gone. Abby walking on wet sand toward the ocean for the first time, screeching at waves splashing her toes while Sheila swam out beyond the breakers. The low sun dimmed and perched on twilight waves.

Then, one afternoon out on the patio, Sheila slid open the back door. I followed her in.

The house smelled of baked salmon, cauliflower, potatoes. Abby cooed from the high chair again. I scooped the unopened mail and two dozen sympathy cards from the table, tossed them on the couch.

Sheila said grace. I didn't bow my head or close my eyes as she thanked God for things. This food, our health, our family. Dear heavenly father. In your name.

I held Sheila in my arms and told her how I'd changed, how I considered every day the greatest gift.

We could live in Japan and Abby would become bilingual, and when we returned, she'd be the smartest kid in school. We'd make Sheila's dreams happen, sell the house and buy one in her hometown so Abby could love on her grandparents.

I was finally listening to her, see? I might've been hearing her for the first time in my life, but I promised I'd never stop.

"Stay," I whispered.

But she wouldn't stay. Not even in my dreams.

I flipped to the inverse of myself, the shadow of love. I became the hole, the absence of light, the sucking at the center of galaxies. A place only death escapes.

                                                    Max Hipp

My calls forwarded to voicemail until the box filled. When deliveries came, I cracked the door and took the boxes of groceries, quarts of wonton soup, pizzas, and stapled wax-paper pharmacy bags.

I studied interesting facts on the internet:

Ingesting large quantities of Xanax with large quantities of alcohol can result in asphyxiation and death.

Idling vehicles in closed garages for extended periods of time can result in carbon monoxide poisoning.

The state of Georgia requires no waiting period between the retail purchase and delivery of handguns.

I was still in pajamas, expecting a shipment of disposable plates and cutlery, when the knock came.

I opened the door and a floppy black shoe landed on the threshold. Then came a rubber chicken's head, crazily wobbling, with a tattered valise closed on its neck.

An airhorn blasted in my face and I fell against the wall, covering my ears.

The clown bounded into the room and dropped the case and bindle. He frowned, twisting his fists under his eyes, poking out his bottom lip at me.

"Goddammit!" I said.

He shrugged and extended his card. He picked up his belongings and kicked a trail through the trash to the extra bedroom.

The card said PERIWINKLE.

Next morning, I was eating Cocoa Puffs on the patio when he came out in full makeup. He offered me a flower and water squirted up my nose. I slapped him, he slapped me back, I slapped, he slapped. Enraged, I picked up a chair and fell backward into the flowerbed. He went to his knees, his white mouth hanging open as his head bobbed in silent laughter at me.

One night the fire alarm sounded. I opened my bedroom door, setting off a Rube Goldberg contraption that burst a water balloon on my head.

He kept heating cans of beans on my hot plate. His flatulence smelled like burning tires.

These were distractions, but humans muddled through jobs, cars, phones, games, porn, kids' school plays, amusement parks, music, rodeos, clowns. Whole lifetimes of distractions. What was life but distraction from death?

After days of takeout and beans, three boxes arrived. I scowled at him for making purchases with my laptop. He pulled out a new velour jacket and kicked it around in the backyard.

One box contained only greasepaint, fake teeth, whoopee cushions. The last one held a black suit, black bowler, patent leather shoes. The suit's coat fit me. The pants' hem swallowed the shoes. When I put on the hat he jerked me out the back door and shoved me down in the grass, kicked dirt on my clothes. He dusted his hands and bowed.

"You're the worst," I said, getting up.

He stuffed cards in my pocket. I pulled one out. LAST YEAR'S MAN it read. "What kind of name is that?"

He shrugged.

The last morning, Periwinkle put on his porkpie hat. He pulled out a pocket watch with an enormous face, its hands spinning. His jaw dropped in feigned surprise. Frantically, he finger-walked the tiny pants across the table.

My throat tightened.

"You're leaving?"

He pretended to steer an enormous wheel. He squat-walked around the kitchen, pumping his arms and blowing a wooden whistle.

I smeared on the white greasepaint and used Sheila's makeup to pencil a thin mustache. I drew a fat comma tear under each eye. With hat, coat, etc., I was convincing.

We were far out of the city before he signaled to stop. He collected his bindle and valise from the trunk and waved for me to follow.

Railroad tracks the other side of the tree line. A long horn blew in the distance. A train pulling graffiti-free cars, the only clean cars I'd ever seen, began creeping around the bend spewing thick smoke.

He ran alongside an open car, moving well in floppy shoes, tossing in his belongings. He caught the siderail and hoisted himself up. He cast his imaginary fishing line at me, started reeling.

I'd been pretending there was something in the house to return to. But what did it mean to leave? I decided to stop worrying what things meant. Meaning had left me this: A train gaining speed.

I ran to the caboose and struggled onto the platform, my heart chugging in my chest. The rails sang beneath me.

The world tilted into pastures, rivers, twilight, stars.

ACKNOWLEDGMENTS

Thanks to the following people who were kind enough to read some of these stories in previous drafts and tell me what they thought. What a wild gift.

KLM: KC Mead-Brewer and Lenore Willow.

Beyond Bud: Alan Ten-hoeve, Kayla Jean Murphy, Nikki Volpicelli, Ishaan Goel, Chuckry Vendagam, Denise Robbins, Mike Lauer, Bud Smith, and Felisha Urso.

Home team folks: David Shirley, Tyler Keith, Jimmy Tighe, Tracy Morin, Riley Manning, Julia Blake, Ryan Pierce, Jasmine Karlowski, Mary Miller, and Lucky Tucker.

Writer Camp/Barrelhouse: Ken Wohlrob, Ben Gwin, Dave Housley, Sam Ashworth, Jonathan Crowl, and Rachele Krivichi.

Shout out to Daniel Fyffe for creating accompanying and inspiring artwork as I drafted "Last Year's Man" for *7x7*.

Special thanks to Susan Bauer Lee and Tim Lee for making incredible things happen wherever they go. Without them, this book would still be on my laptop.

Big thanks to my family for their support and encouragement. And thanks to my brothers and sisters in rock and roll.